Silly's Mirror

Ho Eun Liberata

iUniverse, Inc.
New York Bloomington

Silly's Mirror

iUniverse books may be ordered through booksellers or by contacting:

iUniverse
1663 Liberty Drive
Bloomington, IN 47403
www.iuniverse.com
1-800-Authors (1-800-288-4677)

ISBN: 978-1-4401-3782-2 (sc)
ISBN: 978-1-4401-3783-9 (ebook)
ISBN: 978-1-4401-3784-6 (dj)

Printed in the United States of America

iUniverse rev. date: 6/5/2009

Before Looking into the Mirror

On a listless autumn day, a child lay beneath the cool shade of a tree as a soft breeze fanned the air. The child appeared to be one who ate well and didn't have a care in the world. She was as innocent as an unbridled pony and had more time and freedom than other children had. However, there was a lot that the child did not have, and this lack was enough to startle many people, who assumed that she must be mentally and physically slow. The child had many nicknames: "Loser," "Idiot," "Sil Sil" (for silly). Of those names, people eventually chose to call the child "Silly," because she always giggled in a silly manner. Silly was always lost in her own musings.

"Silly, I told you to study, but you're sleeping again."
"Mommy, I study while sleeping."

I am Silly, grown up now and musing on my life and the ever-present dreams.

While lying down or thinking absentmindedly about something, I dream. Repetitive and so real, dreams have been the very essence of breathing and moving for me from when I was a child to now. Recurring dreams were ropes that bound me down ever more fiercely the more I resisted.

Why is it like this? Why do I keep dreaming the same dream?

I spent my time wrapped up in such questions. Before I knew it, I had become an adult, started my career, married, and had given birth to a child. I vaguely remember myself going through these changes. My facial expression was teased by some and shunned by others. To hide my true self, I hid behind masks that I truly didn't want to wear, but felt compelled to wear. After adapting my facial expression, I underwent many other changes, some visible, some not. My behavior and personality became insensitive and rigid. And soon, where my thoughts had once roamed freely, I paved an asphalt road over them; I paved this road to support a desire to fill my life up with things.

It was uncomfortable to walk in bare feet, so, I wore comfortable and sturdy shoes to travel on this paved road. And, to get and transport even more stuff, I conducted myself without caring about means or tactics. However, at some point, the asphalt road that I had paved in my thinking became a road that I no longer wished to travel. It became a road where others traveled. Even though I realized this, I was blinded by greed, which compelled me to acquire and fill my life with things. So, I insisted on staying on the road. Every time I got on the paved road, others, with their frightening speed and large size, knocked me over, sending me stumbling down and forcing me to squirm on the ground. My own thoughts had been seized, and like some incapable stranger, I was forced to wander about aimlessly like a gypsy in my own thoughts.

I had many fears and was really a coward. I didn't want to get hurt anymore. So I moved about stealthily and hid in places where no roads led. I didn't pave any new thought roads. In that wandering, I lost consciousness and fell down a bottomless pit.

━━━━━━━━━━

Some time later, I woke up in a small, empty space, through which only air passed. It would have been better had I died, but I had stubbornly opened my eyes and gotten up. As I shivered upon seeing my pathetic self, a weak flickering light appeared and shone on me warmly. I was grateful for its warmth, but sorry it had to see me this way.

"Don't think that it is pitiful, and don't say you are sorry."

I heard a soft echo that seemed as if it would die out at any time.

"Who are you?"

"Who am I? I am your heart, which you tossed aside and didn't bother to look for."

"My heart?"

"I am your heart, which you banished to a distant corner while you worked so hard to pave and widen your road of thoughts. The way you changed from your innocent and fragile self was truly frightening. The sight of you breaking down horrified me. I had just locked the door and was about to turn out the light that I had shone on you. I planned never to shine this light on you again, but then you came to visit me, as you had in the past. You are my master. And although I may not be welcoming my master in a grand room, please know that I am using all my strength to shine all my remaining light of hope on you."

Although I was extremely weak and exhausted, my heart helped me get up from my broken state and regain consciousness. Then it showed me glimpses of the person I had been in the past.

In these visions, the countless roads of thought that I had built were revealed to be nothing but a tangled highway leading nowhere. I, wearing shoes that had lost all usefulness, was running and rushing about like a mad person on an asphalt road of thought. Then, after being sucked into a vortex, I was scrambling frantically, running against the other traffic.

"Oh, my master, please be born again with pure free thoughts and an abundant heart."

The urgent plea of my heart reawakened the last bit of my childlike innocence and pushed me to run forth toward a different place. I burst free from the dark asphalt that I had paved over my thoughts. I kicked off the shoes that dampened my senses and threw them far away. For a long time after that, I focused only on emptying myself of all that I had filled myself with while traveling that road. Then, after dreaming a long hazy dream, I woke up.

━━━━━━━━━━━━━

I quit my job, which I had pursued only for the sake of earning money. I got rid of the many material possessions, which had burdened and blinded me. My thoughts grew vast, and I gained a newfound sense of contentment. I felt a sense of peace. And, once again, I started to dream the same recurring dream that I had dreamed as a child.

I turned myself inside out. And then, I started to recall those stories that I had avoided and pushed away. I located these stories in the recesses of my thoughts and heart and began to write them down. I can say I have somewhat finished for now. I have very little learning, and I lack so much in wisdom. I am ordinary and lacking in so many ways. Since a fool like me wrote something, I can't help but be filled with fear about how others may receive it. But, my thoughts are freer than anyone else's are, and my heart is filled with contentment. It is because I want to share with you the contents of my transformed thoughts and heart that I have recorded my pure and innocent dream. I hope that, like a rainbow that appears in the sky after a rain, my story will be a mirror that reflects on you, inviting bright laughter in a beautiful manner after you wipe away your tears. And, if you have gazed into Silly's Mirror to catch a glimpse of yourself, then you must by all means be transformed from this moment on and shall be so transformed. Let's go! Hoping for your transformation, the story begins.

Your Guide,
Silly Ho Eun

Chapter 1: No Space

Ahh.

Dreaming within a dream. Waking up from a dream to another dream. It's difficult to tell whether that place is in a dream. Time passes in a confused and vague fashion. Even if one wanted to wake from the dream and so pushed forth with all one's strength against that nameless thing that presses down on us, the effort would be in vain. That this dream makes me laugh in a silly manner means ...

In such a dream, I spend a long time. And then, I open my eyes. It is difficult to tell whether this very moment might not also be a part of yet another dream.

Paang!

I have fallen again while sleeping on a wicker rocking chair. Upon awakening, I check my reflection at nearby Boa Lake. I see that there is saliva drooling from the left side of my lower lip and that the wicker has left a distinct red pattern on my face. It looks as if I've been slapped with a board. I wash my face with the cool water and try to comb my hair with water, but my hair is unruly and won't easily settle down.

How long did I sleep? I have to hurry back. Father is not well these days, and I feel bad for him. In light of all that, what am I doing? I find my idling and dawdling so pathetic and hateful that I bash myself in the head.

I stop at the head of the path leading down the hill and drop in at a small, local farm. I have to pick up mushrooms from Granny Chang; earlier I had asked her to have them ready for me. I want to make a mushroom soup for my father, who has lost his appetite lately.

"Granny Chang, are you in?"

I call and call for her, but there is no response.

I go out to her field, only to find that it is filled with pigeons, whose feathers shine brightly like a rainbow in the afternoon sun.

"What brings you here?" A gray cat, whose shiny fur makes it seem clever and not quite intelligent at the same time, asks.

"I asked Granny Chang to put aside some mushrooms for me. Did she go somewhere?"

"Are you, by any chance, Mistress Silly?"

"I am."

"Granny Chang groomed the mushrooms herself and took them to Master Moo."

"Oh, I see," I reply. Then, before I know it, I start walking away, down a short path.

As I pass Granny Chang's small, but tidy, field and am about to leave through a back gate, the hairs on my back quiver and I feel a sudden chill. In the bushes along the side, an eerie sound beckons me closer.

I cautiously pull open the curtain of bushes.

The sound turns out to be a song coming from three bamboo baskets, each covered with a green cloth, a brown cloth, and a gray cloth, respectively.

When I lift up the green cloth, a voice says, "I am Chuhree. I never thought that there was too little room. I have wings but just decline to fly."

I take a deep breath and put my ears closer to the bamboo basket.

"I enjoy my life with them. I am a peaceful spirit who lives on as time and lays eggs in this area."

Then, a heavy and frightening sound comes from the basket covered by brown cloth. When I touch the brown cloth to lift it up, purple bruises appear on my hand. I am overcome with pain. The sound coming from the basket is akin to a shrill song of distress.

"I am Jiri. I hate myself, and I hate my ancestors even more. Day in and day out, my lot is to follow a path that I didn't even choose."

I feel sadness and sorrow that is more intense than anything I've ever felt before.

"There is a me who lies with sickness on a small floor. There is a me who is also sick and who lays on top of that other me and takes short breaths. There is another me who steps on them both and stands tall. Those beings of the flesh that lack a sense of existence make their existence known through death. Hard labor is nausea, confusion, and pain, which reveals itself every time one eats something, as one's body becomes bloated even while there is no real sensation. My sickened spirit and flesh become curses on them."

Listening to this song, I also feel a pain spread through my body.

"Who's there?"

My eyes meet those of the gray cat, and then I sheepishly touch its nose.

"I heard the singing—"

Startled, I take a step back and nearly fall.

Even from a quick glance, it is clear that the gray cat's face has turned pale.

"Mistress Silly, have you seen it?"

"Seen what? I heard a song, so I moved closer to hear it."

"So that's what happened."

I am so startled that my body is shivering, and I am having cold sweats. The gray cat motions for me to wait a moment and then hands me some water.

"Please drink this."

Once I drink the water that the gray cat gives me, my body feels awakened and refreshed. The dark bruises on my hand, as well as the accompanying pain, disappear. I make a fist and then open my hand. There is no longer any sign of injury.

"Why in the world am I standing here like this?" I murmur to myself.

The gray cat laughs coarsely and says, "You said you were going to see Master Moo."

"Ah, that's right! Anyway, I'm busy," I say abruptly. Then I race home quickly, all the while struggling to catch my breath. Once home, I see an indescribably brilliant light seeping out of Father's window.

It seems Granny Chang has already gone back to her home.

Hurriedly, I open the door and go inside. My father, who is sitting in a chair near the window, speaks to me in a thick and low voice.

"I already ate dinner. Silly, go ahead and rest. You've worked hard."

It is what he always says to me.

That evening, I again suffer throughout the night from high fever and nightmares. I fall repeatedly down a chasm that seems to have no bottom, and every time, someone who seems to have been waiting for me catches me.

I wake up soaked in sweat.

"I'm dizzy."

The room, which is hazy and unclear, gradually becomes clear. On the nightstand next to the bed, there remains a trace of someone having nursed me through the night.

Earthenware

The window ledge fills up with an unquantifiable sense of joy, so I open the window all the way. It feels as if a firecracker is exploding. In a sudden flash, all my sleep is dispersed far and wide. I hear soft footsteps.

It's Father.

As soon as I get up from bed, Father enters the room, holding small clay bowls in both hands.

"You're up! Silly, come here and take these bowls."

I hurry off the bed and take the two small bowls from Father.

They are small, but each is distinct from the other in its own way. One is rough. The other is extremely fine.

"Father, this bowl ..." I say to Father, but my voice trails off before finishing the question.

"The table in your in your room seemed empty, so

I brought these to brighten things up a bit. Which one is better?" he asks.

"The rough one is good in its roughness. The fine one is good in its fineness. So you pick, Father."

"It'll go on the table in your room, so it should suit you. What use is it if it suits me? Let's keep both them here for a few days. Then, pick the one you like and remove the other one." Father then leaves the room, quietly closing the door behind him.

I quickly get dressed and go down to the kitchen. Jabez is there, surrounded by the scent of mung beans and absorbed in his cooking.

I try to sneak up on him without a sound to startle him, but Jabez suddenly turns around and stomps his foot on the floor, making a loud *koong!*

I am so startled; I nearly collapse on the floor.

Perhaps Jabez is startled by my being startled. He comes toward me and asks, "Are you okay, Master Silly?"

"It's fine! Jabez, can I help you with anything?"

Jabez smiles brightly. "Master Moo already ate and went out to the field. Now it's Master Silly's turn to eat."

While eating Jabez's delicious mung bean porridge, I notice a small vase on the table.

"Jabez, this vase wasn't here before."

"Master Moo brought it this morning. He had me choose one of two vases. After a lot of stressful thinking, I picked this one."

"Jabez, I also received two bowls from Father to put on my table. He asked me to pick one, but I couldn't. So he told me to keep both for a few days and then to get rid of one."

"Ah, you must have received the morning dew bowls."

"What are morning dew bowls?" I ask.

Jabez replies. "It's like this: if you use the bowls to catch morning dew drops one drop at a time, the scent of life will collect on them and spread. The bowls are small but very precious, Master Silly."

"Morning dew bowls!"

I finish the rest of my breakfast quickly and go out with Jabez to the field.

Up ahead, Father is bent over at the waist, already working the field.

Whenever I set foot inside Father's small plot, it feels indescribably large. That large size shocks me. And that sense of shock soon fills me with awe. However, as I follow Father around and work, before I know it, my body and heart become light. It is all a truly marvelous experience.

After helping out in the field, Jabez and I go fishing in Boa Lake. On the way back from the lake, I stop in again at the small, local farm and give some fish to Granny Chang.

Then I go to bed and fall asleep earlier than I do on other nights.

The next day, I get up and quietly go out to the backyard in my bare feet into the crisp, pure dawn. I carefully gather the morning dew that clings to the petals and leaves, and then come back inside to my room.

Inside the rough bowl, I place one drop of dew. Then, without even realizing what I'm doing, I place many more drops in the fine bowl. The room quickly fills up with the scent of life.

But then, strangely enough, whether it is due to the fine bowl being so pretty or due to my strange desire to fill the bowl, the dewdrops fill up the fine bowl and spill over. The outside surface of the bowl gets soaked and becomes covered with a dusky mildew, which produces an unpleasant odor. For the next two days, a strange compulsion to fill the fine bowl forces me to continue to add dewdrops into that overflowing bowl. Without fail, the dewdrops spill over and feed the mildew, which continues to give off a foul odor. In the end, I put aside my sentimentality and summarily remove that fine bowl from my table.

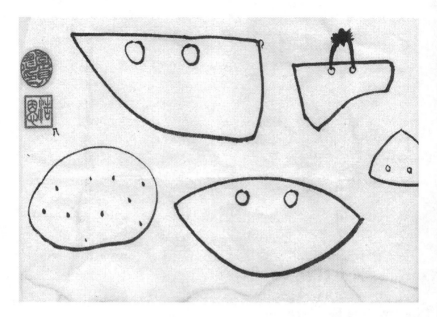

Dead Tree

Out on a hike, Father and I pass the Hong Ah Flower Road and continue toward the forest. The invigorating scent of the woods clears and cools our minds. The forest floor, which is uneven and rough, makes walking difficult, but is rich and good for the forest's well-being.

Father always says the same thing when he walks through the woods.

"Be careful you don't blaze a trail at any old place, and don't step on things."

He walks in front in his bare feet, and his steps are as light as a feather.

The scent of wet moss comes at us from a different direction.

As always, we sit on a dry, sun-drenched stone, catching our breath and resting our bodies. All the many things that make up a forest bloom and peak in their own time, but there is an overall order. In no time at all, the separate parts all find their own proper place and together build a healthy forest. In the midst of flowers, grasses, and trees, which stand together in a knoll, we spot a rotted tree that is still standing.

Father asks, "What purpose do you think that rotted tree is serving?"

Caught by surprise, I answer, "A rotted tree serves no purpose."

Father asks, "Why does it serve no purpose?"

I answer, without much thought, "Because it is rotted. With rotted wood, we cannot build a house. Neither can we use it to sculpt. It's not even suitable as fuel to feed a fire."

"I see. This is what you think about this? It's true that if a thing rots, then it becomes difficult to find a use for it. But there are many things that I purposely leave in place so that they will rot."

I shake my head to show that I don't understand.

"Father, you have told me in the past that living things are good to look at and that anything with life also holds hope."

"You are right. You have quite a memory. Anything living that has life also holds hope. But, Silly, I want to ask you one more thing. Where do you think hope comes from?"

"Isn't it likely that it comes from some tiny thing?"

"And what do you think that thing is?"

"I'm not sure."

My voice trails off. I lower my head and rub the surface of the stone with my bare foot.

Father speaks again. "We can find out all things if we turn them over."

He then gets up from the stone and saunters into the thick forest.

I continue to sit on the stone and stare for a long while

at the rotted tree. The area around the rotted tree is greener and fresher than other areas.

"Once a thing rots, it's useless."

"It's not important whether to rot is useful or useless."

"Since something has rotted, it must, in its own way, continue to rot and disappear."

"Therefore, to rot is …"

I must have sat like that for a while, as thoughts drifted about in my head before falling asleep again.

"Silly, get up now and go. Jabez is calling you from down over there."

"Yes."

When I lift my stiff and heavy eyelids, I am in a resplendent heaven.

I yawn, lift my body up, and pat the dust off my behind. Father walks over to me gently and kisses me on the forehead as he whispers, "Good, Silly."

Father's kiss helps me get up.

As I walk down out of the dense and rough forest, a sense of longing makes me turn back and look at the rotted tree again. At the same time, a bright green leaf on a nearby tree says good-bye to me in a dignified manner.

I return the farewell with a soft laugh.

Today is the same as always. The path I take down the forest is a path that I do not know at all.

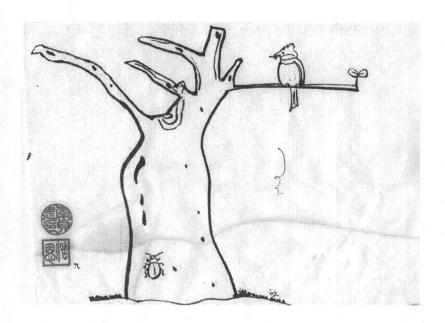

Water

The area around Boa Lake is always peaceful and overflowing with life. The edge of the lake where the water is shallow is filled with big and small rocks. Even though the rocks appear similar, there is a difference between the ones that touch the water and those that don't touch it. I swim from Loyalty Rock to the purplish garden that is filled with irises. I swing my arms wide and welcome my meeting with the water. I sense this feeling of welcome from the top of my head to the tips of my feet.

As I draw closer to the Purple Light Garden, an intense aroma and light make my head hot. I must quickly step out of the water. My wet clothes should be dry by now, but water continues to drip from them. It is as if the water is so glad to see me that it doesn't want to part. It clings to my body ever so closely.

The song of the lark is particularly pleasant to hear. In the distance, I can see the lily garden, filled with the trumpet of angels, and the Rainbow Woods. Also visible is the grape tree that has no worries.

However, the grape tree that has no worries looks strangely lifeless, and its leaves are parched.

"What's going on?"

The grape tree with no worries, that has always had fresh leaves and thick clusters of grapes, now looks dried up, as if it were a dead tree. As I tear off the dried leaves and groom the vines, I sense death: the tree is completely devoid of a life force.

"What should I do? What exactly happened to you, the grape tree that has no worries? That's it! Water. I must give it water."

I take off my wet clothes and wring them out over the tree. Thus, I give water to the tree. Staring at the grape tree that has no worries, I realize that I have been too inattentive to it. I simply can't turn around and go home just now.

I hold the tree tightly in my arms and whisper, "I send my life energy to you. I send it to you."

Meanwhile, Jabez's voice draws closer and closer.

"Master Silly. Master Silly!"

Still holding on to the grape tree, I tell Jabez of my remorse.

"My dear friend, it seems the grape tree with no worries is dead."

The expression on Jabez's face quickly changes as he takes turns staring at me and then at the tree quizzically.

"Silly, you should get up and go now."

Father appears from behind Jabez, who is still turning his head from me to the tree and back.

Seeing Father, I am overwhelmed by a sudden sadness. I let go of the grape tree and run to Father.

"Father, the grape tree that has no worries …"

Father stretches out his two arms, gently holds my

shoulders, and slowly turns me back toward the tree. I can't help but doubt my eyes. The grape tree with no worries is now filled with brilliant grapes and is shining brightly.

"Father, just a moment ago, this tree was all dried up and looked as if it were dead."

"That grape tree is full of the water of life. Did you give it water?"

"Yes, I did give it water, but … it was water that I wrung out of my wet clothes."

Father speaks again. "Water is life. It is a precious and mysterious thing."

Then, Father goes to the grape tree.

"A tree, whatever may be the case, has hope. Even when it is fallen, it can sprout again and grow again. Even when its roots grow old in the soil, even when parts of it die buried underground, as long as it tastes water, it can grow again as if it were a young sapling."

As Father blesses the grape tree with no worries, I think about water.

"Water is hope."

Father's Barley

On an afternoon that was filled with an unusually pleasant scent of herbs, when the sky was full of fluttering butterflies fluttering, Father, who was drinking tea in the field, quietly called for Jabez and me.

On top of a table made of aromatic wood sat two jars, two sacks of barley, and two walnuts.

"Silly and Jabez, come and sit here."

Father's resonant voice was especially pleasant to the ear.

"I harvested these. I want to give them to you as a gift."

Jabez put his hands together and said, in a quivering voice, "But these are such precious things ..."

"There is nothing in this world that is not precious and

valuable. But, you two are far more precious to me than these things, so I have no regrets about giving them to you. All that is in these sacks is yours. First, put the walnuts in the jars, and then put in the barley."

These things that Father grew and harvested personally were priceless. Even one morsel was valuable enough to trade for any other thing that existed in the world. Yet, Father was telling us that a jar filled with these things would be ours soon. Naturally, Jabez and I rushed without a moment's hesitation to fill the jars with barley.

After filling his jar to the brim with barley, Jabez looked down and spoke softly.

"Master Moo, I've filled it."

"Good. This then is Jabez's jar and barley."

"Father, I, too, am done filling."

Father looked at my jar. It was only about half full of barley.

"Good. This then is Silly's jar and barley."

Then Father put both jars on the ground.

"Give the walnuts to me, and keep the barley. Barley that falls on the ground belongs to the ground. Barley that remains in the jar truly belongs to you," said Father.

I put my hand in the jar, took out the walnuts, and gave them to Father.

At that moment, Jabez's jar tipped over. Jabez had packed his jar tightly to the brim with barley. Hence, he couldn't get his hand through to dig out the walnuts. As he struggled with the jar, more and more barley fell to the ground. Then Jabez lost his balance and fell, tipping the jar over with him.

Lifting the jar and setting it back upright, the now-despondent Jabez got up from the ground.

"Father, would it be all right if I shared mine with Jabez?"

Father, who had been staring at Jabez, said, "It is yours to do with what you like." Then he left the field.

The barley that had fallen on the ground seeped instantly into the earth.

I held up Jabez's empty jar and said, "Jabez, don't fret. I have nothing that I truly desire or need. Take all my barley."

Jabez kissed my hand warmly. "I have already received something that is far more valuable than this precious barley," he said, and then went inside to the kitchen.

I set my jar containing the barley on the table, and then poured the contents carefully back into Father's barley sack.

At the Market

Jabez woke me up early and then busily went up and down the stairs. He called out to Father in an excited voice, "Master Moo, everything is ready."

"Jabez, you did well. Go and bring Silly."

I went down the stairs and said in a loud voice, "Father, Silly, too, is ready."

Father, Jabez, and I then got on Chyo Chyo Syong.

I had given the mobile carriage the name Chyo Chyo

Syong because it arrived at our doorstep in the time it took to blink an eye. All we had to do to hail it was call out Chyo Chyo twice.

The carriage was a vessel that belonged to Father. From the outside, it looked small, but when you got on, it was very spacious and magnificent.

Jabez led me to a chair that was to Father's left. Going with Father on a somewhat rare outing to Won Ro Won Square was enough to fill me with excitement.

"Silly, give me your hand."

Father held my hand, and then put a Senium into my pocket.

"You never know. So hold on to that."

Then, he whispered softly to Jabez. "Jabez, you have to make sure you are constantly by Silly's side."

When we got off at the center of Won Ro Won Square, many races of people wearing brown traditional ethnic garb fell on their knees and showed tribute to Father.

Jabez quickly grabbed my hand, led me around to the back of Chyo Chyo Syong, and then toward the market.

The shops were filled with various sorts of marvelous items. Shops displayed goods such as water, soil, light, seeds, minerals, and souls. Many races were making transactions, including the people of the Sang Kah tribe, who looked quite rough and had abundant minerals to sell in their mineral shops.

A group of Mo Gu Rim people were buying soil. It seemed as if they were not doing well. They seemed to be pleading with the merchant for some sympathy.

Holding Jabez's hand, I went closer to the group of Mo Gu Rim people.

"How are you?"

The group of Mo Gu Rim people turned their large bodies to me. They seemed to be startled to see me. They lowered their heads and spoke to me in a clumsy and slow fashion.

"Mistress Silly!"

"The Mo Gu Rim tribe knows me!" I thought to myself as I glanced over at Jabez.

At the same moment, Jabez asked the owner of the shop what was going on.

The shop owner explained that the Mo Gu Rim people did not have enough Da Mon to barter for the amount of soil that they had originally ordered. Hence, the shop owner was trying to figure out what to do. Both the shop owner and the Mo Gu Rim people seemed to be very perturbed by their situation and were staring at one another.

I reached into my pocket and took out the Senium, which was the size of a grain of barley. Once I'd taken out the Senium, a murmur arose from some distance, where the Sang Kah tribe was bartering.

The large Mo Gu Rim people took a step back in unison and seemed not to know what to do.

The shop owner seemed even more perplexed. He insisted that he could not accept the Senium from me. He then immediately asked me how much soil he ought to give to the Mo Gu Rim people.

I didn't know what all the fuss was about and turned to Jabez, but Jabez remained still with his head lowered.

The Mo Gu Rim people handed the shop owner a satchel. The shop owner put the soil in a container, and then placed the container in the satchel.

Staring at the container, I asked the Mo Gu Rim people.

"Mo Gu Rim, why do you need so much soil?"

The biggest of the group explained the need for soil.

"Master Silly, soil is the food and shelter of the Mo Gu Rim people. There's always a shortage, and we are always in dire need of it."

I again looked upon the Mo Gu Rim people and said, "Mo Gu Rim, I understand that there is lacking and dire need. But next time you come to the market to barter for goods, please make sure you have prepared enough Da Mon for fair bartering."

As soon as I was done speaking, Jabez whispered to me.

"Other tribes are right now coming in droves to you, Master Silly. Things may get awkward here, so it's best that we leave now."

Indeed, just as Jabez had described, people from various tribes were coming from everywhere toward me.

"I think we should do as you say."

Jabez grabbed my hand, and quickly led me out the back door of the shop and back toward the Square.

Hurrying, we quickly passed the edge of the market. Up ahead, we could see Chyo Chyo Syong parked at Won Ro Won Square.

Struggling to catch our breath, we got back on the mobile vessel. Father was sitting on a chair. I remained quiet and worried that Father might find out about the little commotion that Jabez and I had stirred up back at the market. Father smiled at me and rubbed my back. This quickly calmed me.

"Silly, you did well. But, you are still very young, so it is dangerous. Please be careful." He then turned to Jabez. "Jabez!"

"Yes, Master Moo. We will be careful."

As soon as we got back home, Father went out to the field and Jabez went to the kitchen. I followed Jabez into the kitchen.

"Jabez, why did the shop owner back there ask me how much soil he should give to the Mo Gu Rim people? And why would he not accept the Senium from me?"

"All things belong to Master Moo. Who is Master Silly's father?" He flashed me a beaming smile and then went about his work, stirring a pot of resin.

Kiddy Lamp

After turning on the kiddy lamp, I sat opposite Father, reading a book. When I was little, Father would read to me under the light of the kiddy lamp. The kiddy lamp used to make me so happy then. And it still did.

I stopped reading for a while and stared at the kiddy lamp. Staring at it made me feel all warm. Soon, the light from the lamp made me feel ticklish.

"Ha, ha, ha …"

"Silly."

"I'm sorry. It's just that looking at the kiddy lamp makes me feel happy, Father!"

"It is the same for me."

I had expected him to scold me for fooling around while reading, but Father's face was filled with kindness.

"Father, does that kiddy lamp also make you feel ticklish?"

Father turned to the kiddy lamp and then back to me. He then responded, "That kiddy lamp must give you the tickles." He closed his book and moved closer to me. "My Silly is figuring things out one by one."

I was curious why Father was saying that I was figuring things out when the only thing I had done was mention that the kiddy lamp made me feel ticklish.

"What is it that I am figuring out?"

Father pointed to the kiddy lamp. As he did so, a powerful shiver emanated from the lamp.

"Silly, that kiddy lamp is called sunlight," he said, looking at me.

"The kiddy lamp's name is sunlight?" If that was the case, I wondered why Father had told me until then that it was called kiddy lamp.

"Father, then why …"

Father made a face that said he already knew what I was

about to ask him, and then said, "Since you were little, you would see the sun and call it kiddy lamp. Its proper name is sunlight, but I also enjoyed hearing the name you gave it. So, between you and me, we have been calling it kiddy lamp."

"Father, from now on, I will call it sunlight instead of kiddy lamp. The name sunlight allows us to feel more warmth."

Father, who was staring at the sun, spread his arms out wide and said, "Sunlight is a blessing for which we are grateful. Living and being able to see the sun adds joy to our days. Always remember that joy, lest the sun, the moon, and the stars lose their brilliance and the rain brings with it dark clouds."

I suddenly recalled the time Father and I were cleaning mirrors. Father had been cleaning a green mirror when he'd said, "Their greed will blanket the sunlight."

"Father, when we were cleaning mirrors, you said that their—"

Jabez rushed into the room before I could finish my question.

"Master Moo, the doctors from Won Ro have come to see you."

Father cleared his throat and stepped outside.

Jabez began tidying up the books that were piled on the desk. I helped him tidy up the books.

"Jabez, do you know what that is hanging up there?"

Jabez looked up at what I was referring to and said, "That is sunlight."

Green Mirror

Jabez goes out early to the cornfield on an errand for Father.

"It's still early, but I'm going to prepare a meal in Jabez's place," I murmur to myself as I hurry out of bed.

However, the kitchen is already filled with the pungent fragrance of wild sesame seeds.

Granny Chang is there, wiping the dining table.

"Hello, Granny Chang!"

Granny Chang sees me and bows as if she is delighted to see me.

"Master Silly, you've gotten up early. I've prepared wild sesame porridge."

She pulls out a chair for me, and then says, in a soft voice, "Master Moo left a note for you. Master Silly, would it be okay for me now to go back up to my farm?"

She has worked hard from very early in the morning. I try to stand up and see her off, but she simply steps back without any fanfare.

"Thank you for your hard work. Please go home now."

Granny Chang opens the side door that leads out from the kitchen, steps out, carefully shuts the door behind her, and then sets off back to the farm.

On the table, there is wild sesame porridge and a note written on pine tree paper.

"I have arranged for Jabez to look after the field work. I have to attend a meeting at Won Ro and will not be home for a few days. Please clean the mirrors for me."

It is a short message.

After I am done with a fair amount of the chores, I open the door to Father's room. Numerous mirrors of various sorts are strewn about the room. As I always do when I step inside Father's room, I suddenly feel a limitless strength. Of the many mirrors in the room, I know that Father especially cares for the green mirror that is made of dirt and is hidden behind the curtain.

Inside, I am quite nervous. I've cleaned mirrors with Father a few times, but I've never done it before by myself.

The mirrors that are behind the red mirror must be cleaned with a long pole. The mirrors around the brown mirror must be shaken about with a piece of cloth. And I think the purple mirror and a few others need to be cleaned by blowing gently on them.

I gingerly clean the mirrors. Then, at last, I draw the curtains aside and stand before the green mirror.

I pull a chair made out of gingko wood toward the mirror and wonder, "What would happen if I used a long pole or a piece of cloth to clean this mirror?"

I am truly very curious.

I nervously grab the pole. Then, as soon as the pole touches a part of the green mirror …

━━━━━━━━━━━━━━

At the foot of a mountain near a shallow river upon which reeds and river grasses danced, a brown bear was trying to catch fish. The bear's basket was empty. And the worn-out appearance of the bear's face made it clear that it had suffered from hunger.

"Try a different spot."

"Do I look dumb? This spot here is a famous spot. People can come here with their eyes closed. But, then again, my oldest brother and my second oldest brother did go out looking for another road …" The brown bear paused to take a deep breath, and then got up and started to go away. "If it's like this here, then other places must be the same."

After parting from the brown bear, I soon found myself deep in the forest, at a place so packed with trees that no sunlight shone through them.

A gray bear had its paws in a beehive to get honey. A swarm of bees was all over the bear, stinging it. It was difficult to tell whether the bees were eating the bear or the bear was eating the bees' honey.

After a while, the gray bear's body swelled up from the stings, and then the bear slowly went over to the shade under a tree inside a thin gap between some boulders. I wanted to ask the bear whether it was okay, so I followed it. The bear was startled and began lamenting its fate.

"In search of food, I left my younger brother and came here with my older brother. My older brother went away to look for another place. I am alone now and have been collecting honey here."

Lurking in the shadow like that, the gray bear seemed coarse and grumpy.

"This forest is dark and wet. I am sick of these densely packed trees and the swarms of bees! But, then again, no other place has honey as sweet as the honey here."

The bear, which had griped so much, then turned around and took a nap.

I didn't want to disturb the bear's nap, so I carefully walked away and climbed up to the mountaintop.

There, I caught my breath and looked all around me. A green bear was leaning against a boulder. The worried expression on the green bear's face seemed truly grave.

"Are you worried about something?"

"I know this area really well. I've been going up and down this mountain. So I know which lake is fresh and which lake is dry. I know the spots that get plenty of sunshine, even in the midst of the dark forest. I know this all from coming up here to the peak. I have learned from being able to see everything."

"I envy you that you know this mountain so well. But then, if that is so, why do you have such a dark and gloomy expression?"

"I keep seeing my younger brothers in my head."

"Ah! Then your younger brothers must be the brown bear and the gray bear whom I met on my way up here."

"You met my younger brothers? How are they?"

"I'm not sure."

"I want to tell my younger brothers that there is a place that is plentiful and good."

"Then you can go down and tell them."

"Actually, I now have a family of my own. If I leave this place, something bad might happen to them. That's why I am stuck here unable to do this or that."

As I took a step toward the green bear, my foot caught on a tree branch. I lost my balance and fell down a cliff.

How much time passed? I do not know.

Awakened by a sharp pain, I opened my eyes to find myself lying on a swampy bank near a lake. I remained like that for a long time. I lay on reeds and watched the clouds pass over me.

"*Quack. Quack.*"

A flock of ducks was headed toward me.

"Do you remember when that was? There was a frost coming down, and we were moving downstream. We ran into a storm and had such a hard time."

"I remember. I thought we were all going to die from hunger."

"Yes, there was a strange smell coming from the water. It was foul."

"That's all fine and good, but when do we head out?"

"Hey, don't you think that one over there with the stripe on his neck is really fashionable?"

I couldn't help but try to join in the ducks' lively conversation.

"Hello, how are you? I am called Silly."

The ducks' eyes were shaking in a strange way. My greeting, which was made in the spirit of fellowship, sent the ducks scattering away. A feather, one of many that fell as the ducks dispersed so quickly, landed on my head.

I should get up, I thought to myself.

I held on to a tall reed and pulled myself up. The flock of ducks returned to me. With a serious glint in their eyes, they said something to me. This was jumbled up with the sound of my feet stepping on the mucky mud on the ground, the sound of other ducks swimming about some distance away, and the sound of tall reeds scratching one another. All together, they formed and told their own story.

Then, the flock of ducks gathered above my head and set off into the sky, dancing in military formation.

Eventually, I managed somehow to find my way out of the swamp. Along the way, I was overcome with fear and shivering. It had been difficult to walk through the swamp, and my mind was neither comforted nor refreshed.

Up ahead, I saw a cluster of trees.

I should dry my wet clothes, I thought to myself.

But strangely enough, I found that the warm rays of sunlight stung and my wet clothes had changed color from white to black. Feeling strange, I looked about me.

"Keh, Kehng!" There was a shrill cry. I searched for the source of the sound.

Two baby foxes and a mother fox were next to a large boulder.

The mother fox kept biting the babies' necks, letting go, and kicking the baby foxes, over and over.

The tiny bodies of the baby foxes were covered in blood, and they were dying! It was an incomprehensible scene. Outraged, I picked up a sharp stick from the ground, rushed madly toward the mother fox, and struck her on the head with it.

"This can't be!"

On the necks of the baby foxes were metal traps. And strewn all about were the mother fox's broken teeth and claws and the great amount of blood that had poured out of the mother fox's teeth and claws. It was a sadness colored in red.

I quickly removed the metal traps from the necks of the baby foxes, and then touched their necks. Fortunately, they were still breathing. The mother fox had lost a lot of blood and was breathing weakly.

With shivering hands, I picked up the traps and thought about what had just taken place.

What was it that I saw a short while ago from the cluster of trees? And what is this that I see now? How could a conclusion that I drew from something that I saw with my own eyes turn out like this?

I was very confused, but I needed to be focused.

The injuries on the baby foxes were serious, and the condition of the mother fox was also not good. I thought about how best to treat the mother and her babies. Then I remembered wild sage, with which Father had once treated a wound.

I gathered some wild sage from nearby and applied it with care on their wounds. Then I wrapped the wounds with strips of cloth torn from my clothes.

I built a fire and burned wild sagebrush throughout that night, so that the medicinal smoke would help the fox family regain strength and recover. Gradually, night turned to day. To help the fox family quench their thirst, I went to the small stream that I had stumbled upon while gathering wild sage.

I took off my shoes and used them to scoop water from the stream for the fox family. As I did so, drops of water fell on my reflection on the water's surface, breaking up my face. I suddenly felt dizzy and lightheaded.

Father's voice echoed through the air.

"Silly, Silly."

I fell from the chair made of gingko wood.

Father was there, staring intently at me.

I felt wide-awake and got right up on my feet.

"Father, you're back already."

"The meeting was cancelled. You can stop cleaning the mirrors. Go and rest."

I stood there blankly. Father said, "Silly, I am tired and wish to rest." He then sat on a chair.

"Yes, I will then go out to the field."

"We need to give them water."

I didn't know whether it was because it was the first time I'd seen Father so tired or it was because of the mirrors I'd cleaned, but when I, who had never before offered to go out to the field on my own, volunteered to do so, Father looked back and smiled quietly.

For the next few days, Father remained in his room and did his work except during meals. Every now and then, he also went out to the field to do some work there.

At night, he stood about gazing at the backyard and seemed to be worrying about something. Even as I watched my Father at such times, I found myself murmuring to myself, "We need to give them water."

I didn't know to whom we needed to give water or why I kept finding myself repeating this sentence. I was aggravated by not knowing.

Out in the backyard, a bunch of violets that bloomed together appeared to be withered. I got some water and watered them. Afterwards, they were strong and vibrant.

"We need to give them water."

"Silly! You already gave water to the fox family. So you need not worry."

I heard Father speaking to me from the other side of the fence.

"That's right. The foxes were hurt. There were baby foxes and a mother fox!"

Father held my hand, which was still wet from watering, and said softly, "Kind Silly, I can send you away now."

"Send me away? Where to?"

"Without my saying a thing, you will find out in good time. You will see things there. You will dream dreams there. But do not be afraid, Silly! You are weak, so I will make sure you figure things out in small increments. I will protect you from those that are around you."

"Father, are these all things that I can manage? I am worried."

"Do not worry. These are all things that you do best."

"Things that I do best?"

Instead of giving me a spoken answer, Father just nodded.

"You are and will always be here. I am only sending you there temporarily without anyone's finding out about it. If people come to look for you, then I will immediately call you back here. So you need not be puzzled by this."

"Father, I really don't know what's what."

From somewhere, a tiny vortex of light appeared by the window.

"Silly! Go now."

"Father!"

Chapter 2: Beautiful World

Forgiveness

Running madly until dizziness overcame me, I found myself on a hill filled with pine trees. A cluster of pine trees that were slightly taller than I am welcomed me. As I walked past them with my arms spread wide, they greeted me. Each one touched my hand without fail.

As if they understood the truly frightening nature of my mission, these trees cheered for me with their whole being, and the sky cried with me.

I'm not sure what forgiveness is, but I forgive.

"Why did they always hug and smile so warmly at Sister Gina and Jade when they had nothing but hatred for me?"

I cried and threw a tantrum, insisting that Mommy, who was going to the market with Sister Gina, let me go with them as well.

Just then, Daddy came out of the shed.

"I'm here, so don't worry. Go now, and hurry back."

Daddy pointed to the room where Jade was in a deep sleep. My eyes, which had gleamed fiercely during the tantrum, grew weak. I forced myself to shut them. Even as sleep came over me, I heard a soft murmur.

"You're bad luck."

That phrase echoed in my head as I drifted off to sleep.

All of a sudden, a dark valley grew increasingly narrow until it began to squeeze my body. I couldn't breathe. It seemed as if my body stored a certain kind of energy until, at a certain point, this energy began to spread all throughout my body.

A pair of warm hands embraced me.

I coughed as if I were expelling death from my very being. The hands that had embraced me belonged to none other than Mommy.

Mommy was looking at me and shivering intensely. Mommy's heart was beating frighteningly fast and was enough to shake my body. I called for Mommy with all my strength, but no sound came out. My mouth only moved a bit.

"*Mom!*"

She let go of me carefully and started shouting at Daddy.

"What did you do to the child? Are you crazy? Have you lost it? No matter how difficult things get, she is your daughter. You're still a human being. How can you do such a thing?"

"Daddy did this to me ..."

Mommy's hysterical cries awoke Jade.

Daddy stared at me and tried to hug me.

I didn't know where I found the strength, but I kicked open the door and ran outside. My lungs hurt, and I couldn't breathe.

"Silly, Silly!"

The voices of Mommy and Sister Gina resonated softly and came closer to me. The ceiling and walls were filled with bumps and made me nauseous. Mommy, Sister Gina, younger sibling Jade, and Granny Ho Ya, who lived next door, all danced about in a circle. A piece of red cloth covered me.

Buzz. Buzz. I heard the buzzing of a swarm of bees. Their buzzing slowed and slowed. Then, I heard a quiet voice.

"Finally, there's a breath. She will ... live."

It was Granny Ho Ya's voice, growing ever more faint.

I opened my eyes on a bright, white morning.

I could barely make out faces, which slowly grew more sharp right before my eyes. Mommy's haggard face told me just how much she must have worried by my side.

"Silly, Mommy was worried she was going to lose you," said Mommy. I could see that her eyes were red and soaked in tears, even as she turned away, and then back again, and managed a smile.

Her lips were quivering as she continued to speak. "You may not know this, because you're so young. But around the time you were born, your grandmother ran away. Because of this, your grandfather suffered and eventually passed away. Then Daddy's work didn't go well, and our family became very poor. And now, Daddy's body and heart are both hurting very much."

Mommy's voice kept on quivering.

"Daddy is feeling very bad because so many bad things have happened to us at once. He's taken this stress out on you."

Mommy ended her speech as if she had made some sort of confession and awaited absolution. Then, finding herself unable to look at me, she said, "Can you forgive Daddy?"

I didn't know what was what, so I couldn't say anything.

It seemed that Mommy thought that I must not have heard what she'd just said. Indeed, she'd spoken in such a small and soft voice, as if she'd been speaking only to herself. But I had seen her lips move and knew exactly what she had said.

What she'd said was all true. Around Daddy, there were

always packets of medicine. And Daddy ate the medicine at all times, as if the pills were tasty candies.

I really don't know what forgiveness is. But I really love Daddy, Mommy, Sister Gina, and younger sibling Jade. I love my entire family.

Feeling confused and stifled, I ran toward the hill filled with pine trees.

Dummy

My name was Chesed, but most people who knew me did not call me by this name. Instead, they called me Silly.

A smiling face is capable of brightening the mood of any person.

But, the expression on my face was excessively happy.

People assumed I was abnormal and lacking in some way. These people called me Silly because, like some idiot, I went about smiling in a silly manner.

I felt awful inside and lousy that people thought of me that way. So many people called me by this name that I must undoubtedly have been the most famous kid in the neighborhood.

"Hello! How are you?"

Saying hello to people I encountered was an enjoyable thing to do and made me happy.

"Silly, I see you're coming back from school. You're quite late again today."

"Yes."

After school, I often felt very hungry. Enduring my hunger, I kicked open the front door and stepped inside.

"I've come back from school." I shouted out a customary greeting, but no one came out to welcome me home.

I went around to the backyard. Sister Gina and Jade were by the well with Mommy, washing grapes that were soaking in a red rubber container.

Without a word, I ran over, snatched some grapes, and ate them. The juice from the grapes exploded from them and, like a bursting firecracker, left bits here and there on my clothes.

"Hey, Silly. Eat slowly. You're getting stains on your clothes. You dummy."

Sister Gina poked fun at the way I was pigging out on the grapes.

Jade followed her lead and said, "Sister Silly is a dummy."

Suddenly, something got caught in my throat and I started to cough violently.

It was as if through my coughs, I was protesting that I'd been called stupid. In no time at all, I had spat out all the grapes that I had just shoved in my mouth.

Seeing this, Mommy gently started hitting my back.

"You should have eaten slowly, you dummy."

Even Mommy, who I had trusted to be my one ally, had called me a dummy. Her words stung. And before I knew it, tears were pouring down my face. Through tears, I stared at Mommy.

I started to think, *If Mommy, whom I trust the most and who knows me the best, calls me a dummy, then I must really be a dummy.*

Just then, Mommy laughed again as if she had no idea how I felt.

I was so angry that I thought I was going to go mad. But Mommy just kept on laughing right in front of me.

"Silly, you are a dummy."

Sister Gina shouted at me again, as if she were parroting Mommy.

"Silly is a dummy!"

My eyes filled up with tears of resentment.

"Children, Silly truly is a dummy. *Duh* more you see her, the more precious a treasure she becomes to *me.*"

I repeated what she'd said.

"*Duh* more you see me, the more precious a treasure I become to *me.*"

Appearance

There is a house in our village that people can find, even if they don't know the address, simply by asking for the idiot's house. This famous house is our house.

And I am the idiot.

My hair, which grows in clumps as if someone yanked large patches of it out, my reddish head, my face on which there are patches of dry skin, and my yellowish nose all firmly establish my identity as a sub-par being.

Since I have wandered around our village wearing a gourd

bowl on my head and holding a stick, scarcely anyone in our neighborhood doesn't know who I am.

There aren't many kids my age to be friends with in my town. Hence, I often go about playing the boss with dogs, ducks, chickens, and goats. Of course, in doing so, I feel quite proud of myself and think I deserve praise.

My life is thus confined to what is in a small town. But that is all about to change. Tomorrow, I will enroll at a place called school and my life will take a new direction. I cannot wait.

For the past few days, I have walked about the neighborhood carrying a schoolbag packed with pencils and such things. Having done such practice for real school, I am even more happy and excited.

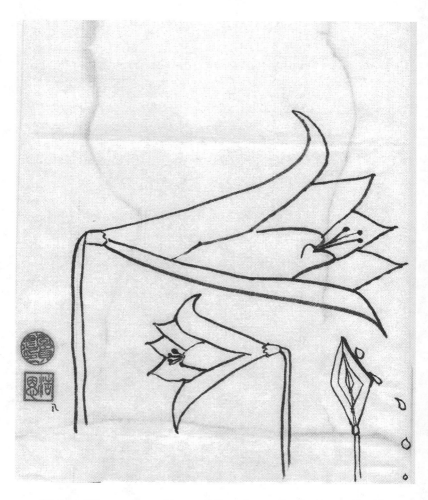

Sister Gina, who always teased me for being stupid and going around with a silly smile on my face, stared at me as if she couldn't make any sense of anything and said, "Silly, if you keep going around like that, other kids will think you're crazy and won't play with you."

All night, I couldn't sleep because I was too excited. I finally managed to fall asleep around dawn, so had trouble getting up.

Sister Gina got tired of trying to wake me up and went

off to school on her own. Mommy had to carry me to school on her back.

The noise of people talking woke me up.

I slid down off Mommy's back.

I stared at Mommy through sleep-filled eyes and said, "Mommy, I have many friends over there."

Mommy pointed to the seats in the front and motioned with her head for me to go there. I took one step after another and marched confidently toward the seats. I hid how nervous I was with a huge smile.

A couple of adults started laughing. Then all my friends suddenly stared at me.

Having so many people stare at me, I froze up like a statue. Mommy rushed to my aid and helped me sit down.

I had no idea what was going. A teacher with an unusually large nose began speaking and gesturing with his hands, but I couldn't tell what he was saying. The only thing I did hear was what I'd heard as I'd tried to walk over to my seat. My ears kept hearing their pronouncements over and over.

"Wow, look at that kid. The kid looks about half-formed. Ha ha."

"Whoever that girl's mom is, she must be really upset."

Piano

I always enjoy playing outside, but on Wednesdays, I wait inside the house filled with excitement.

It's because Granstick Teacher comes that day.

She always winks at me and taps her wand. She sits down at the piano and proceeds to play the pieces that she's been practicing.

"Ding, ding, ding. Dong, dong, dong. Gang, gang ..."

Playing the piano, I dream. Hopping along a flower-filled road, I chase the wind. I run to escape a sudden downpour.

"Your hands are too tense," says Granstick Teacher.

My hands then become soft, like jelly.

One walks for a while before one runs. Likewise, my fingers become rejuvenated and a sound begins to flow from my hands.

Now Sister Gina has her turn.

"Gina, did you even practice?" Granstick Teacher asks.

"Uh ... I did practice."

I am sitting in the courtyard. Sister Gina shoots me a stealthy glance during her piano lesson.

Sister Gina's piano practice ends.

Granstick Teacher has a red scarf wrapped around her neck and is wearing high heels. Every time she sees me playing in the yard, dunking my hands in the red rubber container, she winks at me and walks crisply away.

Sister Gina still is playing the piano.

"Silly!" She calls out, despite her heavy eyelids and her dangling head, which is heavy with sleepiness.

"Sister, I can't see you."

She will push out the piano bench with her butt, stand up abruptly, pack her playthings in a bag, and go to the home of her friend, Sister Ggom Ddu Nae.

"Silly, you know what to do if Mommy comes home, right?"

She then rushes out. From the back, sister looks like a happy duck.

Sister Gina really dislikes three things. They are eating beans, playing the piano, and seeing Granstick Teacher.

Granstick Teacher's real name is Mak Sim, but Sister Gina made a nickname for her. She calls her the Granny with a Stick. So, among ourselves, we call her Granstick.

After Sister Gina leaves, I notice that the piano bench is pushed out and waiting for me, urging me to hurry over. The piano has its mouth open and seems to have been waiting for me for a while. I can't read music, but that's not a problem.

When I hit the keys, my friend speaks to me. The piano and I are friends who have shared so many stories together.

The song I play is the same one that the piano played with Gina, but that's okay.

Even if the song is the same, the person playing is different.

We each become our own unique song. Then, the piano and I play countless songs. My hand starts to hurt. This means it's about time for Mommy to come home.

I close the piano cover and open the front gate.

Sure enough, over in the distance, under the shade of a zelkova tree, there are two shadows.

They are Mommy and Jade.

"Mommy, Jade!" When I run over and pick up the heaviest-looking item from Mommy's grocery basket, Mommy says what she always does.

"Where's Gina?"

Today is just like other days. Like a parrot, I say what I've said before.

"She finished her piano practice and went to Sister Ggom Ddu Nae's house to do her homework."

Conductor

No matter where I have been, people often said that I was lacking in many ways. I think the reason I heard this comment so much was probably that it took me a long time to learn things and, even though I didn't understand much, I talked a lot and said a lot of nonsensical things.

For these reasons, people around us said the following to Mommy.

"If you give Silly too much stress, her mind may become strange. So it's better to just let her be free."

Maybe it was what these people said to Mommy, but whether I chose to read books, watch television, or play outside all day long, Mommy rarely seemed to care what I did, and she almost never told me what to do.

The only thing she demanded of me, reminding me repeatedly, was that I not be lured away by any suspicious strangers.

This was a very easy rule to follow.

Before I could ever go off somewhere with a stranger, strangers would see me and avoid me.

The more that people avoided me, the more I enjoyed watching people and studying them. I learned to mimic the dances and songs of the pop singers on television so well that all the women in the neighborhood would say, "Silly, sing us a song." Every time they asked, it didn't matter where we were, I sang and danced.

When I did so, even passersby would applaud, compliment me, and stroke my head. It seemed like people genuinely liked me, so I was happy.

I thought, *Even I have something I'm good at.*

Our school planned to hold a group singing contest, in which whole classes would compete as a choir.

The teacher picked out a song for our class and selected a conductor. I really wanted to be the conductor. But the teacher chose the class president to be conductor.

I had seen orchestra and choir conductors on television a few times. They looked so cool. Their intensely glistening eyes, vibrantly stirring hands, and dynamically moving shoulders all worked together as they conducted with their entire bodies. This so captivated me that I had found myself mimicking them as I watched without even realizing what I was doing.

Choir practice for the competition started the day after our song and the conductor were chosen. During practice, I imagined myself standing where the class president stood as class conductor.

I am conducting magnificently, I thought to myself.

I was thus conducting enthusiastically in my imagination when a classmate tapped me.

"Silly, why are you shaking your body so much? Just sit still and sing."

I really felt like I was missing out. I couldn't understand how anyone could sing a song like that while just sitting still.

Two days before the choir competition, our class president caught a severe flu.

Our teacher asked, "Who is second-in-charge of extracurricular activities and our choir group?"

My heart beat so fast. It felt as if it were outside my body.

"Silly and Jubilee," my friends answered.

"Silly and Jubilee. I think it'd be good if one of you filled in as the conductor. Who wants to do it?"

Even before the teacher was finished speaking, all my

friends stared right at me. At least, that's how it seemed to me.

As if possessed, my hand shot straight up in the air.

The choir competition was now only a day away.

We went through our last practice. Perhaps I was too nervous, but conducting didn't go as well as I'd hoped. Despite this, my friends encouraged me warmly.

"Silly, your conducting was pretty good."

Then finally, the day of the choir competition came.

After the preliminary introductions, the music teacher explained how the competitors would be judged and the order in which we would go on stage to sing.

Then groups of students took turns going up and down the stage and singing beautifully.

Finally, it was our class's turn. We got on stage and lined up. From the front row to the last row of the stage, we all stood in our blue skirts and white blouses and glistened like lilies about to bloom.

My friends in the choir all stared at me. Their eyes all asked me to lead them. I nodded to them, and then motioned with my head to Je Ru Ga, who was sitting at the piano.

The prelude was played. I was conducting in a relaxed and gentle manner and leading the choir. The rhythm was established. I recalled in my mind all the excellent and magnificent conductors I had seen on television. Using my eyes, my hands, and my entire body, I threw myself into my conducting. I was passionate in my conducting.

Just before we were halfway through our performance, someone in the audience laughed, "Poo hoo." This disrupted us, and our singing became shaky.

Those in our class who were singing just a moment ago were suddenly holding their stomachs and putting their fists in their mouths to try to keep from bursting out in laughter.

I wanted so badly for them to focus. I opened my eyes

wide and frowned to let them know that I was serious. Then, I whispered to them.

"Focus. Why are you getting so distracted?"

Even before I was done speaking, some of my friends plopped down on the stage. It was no surprise that we ultimately stepped off the stage without even finishing our song. That day, our class came in last place in the competition. It was a well-deserved finish.

As we headed back to the classroom, our teacher stopped at the stairwell and pulled me aside.

"Silly, do you know what you did back there?"

I didn't say anything, but I was curious.

What had I done?

Bicycle

Daddy, who had been sick, slowly recovered. He even started to go to work.

Daddy commuted to work by riding a bicycle to the bus station. He'd then leave his bicycle at the scrap metal shop near the bus station and continue his commute on the bus.

Daddy still scolded me frequently and didn't play with me, but strangely enough, instead of disliking him, I thought about him and liked him more than ever.

Of course, Daddy had no idea that this was how I felt about him. But I didn't let that bother me. I'd made up my mind not to let that bother me.

We all gathered together to see Daddy off as he went off to work. Sister Gina saw me and began teasing me.

"You always hang around near Daddy only to get yelled at. So why do you keep lurking around Daddy, you dummy?"

What Sister Gina said was correct, but I didn't pay it any attention. I didn't worry and always saw Daddy off as he headed for work. But even so, Daddy ignored me. He kissed

Sister Gina and Jade, and then hugged Mommy. Then, finally, he waved at Kkori before walking his bicycle out the front door.

After a day at school, I came home to find that Daddy's bicycle was already back.

I stole a glance into Daddy's room. Daddy was lying there with a wet towel on his head. Mommy was massaging his arms and legs.

Seeing Daddy like that, all strength disappeared from me and I plopped down on the floor. Daddy's bicycle, which was in the middle of the front yard, also seemed to be sick.

I will help Daddy get better.

After gathering together the towels that were hanging on the clothesline and grabbing the water bucket, I did what Mommy did and began treating Daddy's bicycle.

With the towel, I wet various parts. I wiped and scrubbed vigorously to remove various dark stains and spots. I worked hard and cleaned Daddy's bicycle.

Envisioning Daddy going to work on his now spotless and shiny bicycle made me feel good again. I was happy because it almost felt as if Daddy was well again.

━━━━━━━━━━

Perhaps it was because of that cleaning, but lately, Daddy hadn't been so sick again. It was such a joyful and fortunate thing.

Today, I was cleaning Daddy's bicycle again.

"Gina!"

Mommy called for Sister Gina.

Muttering, Sister Gina went to Mommy.

"What?"

"Go to Granny Ddee An's store and buy some cheese."

Sister Gina looked around, and then spotted me over in a corner cleaning the bicycle. She came over to me.

"Silly, are you done cleaning the bicycle?"

"Yeah, the only part left to clean is the handle."

"I was in the middle of doing my homework. Last time, you ran like the wind around the playground. Run like that again to Granny Ddee An's store and bring back some cheese."

"Run there like the wind?"

"Yes. While you do that, I'll stay here and clean the handle."

"Okay. Give me money for the cheese. And Silly will go like the wind."

I did run like the wind to Granny Ddee An's store to buy cheese.

Even while waiting for Granny Ddee An to slice the cheese, I kept moving my feet.

"Silly, you're moving about so much that I can't think straight."

"Granny, I am the wind. The wind doesn't stand still."

I took the cheese that Granny Ddee An handed me and ran like the wind back home. I gave the cheese to Sister Gina.

"That was amazing, Silly. You're faster than the wind," she said, flattering me.

Swept up in excitement, I went outside and ran like the wind once around the entire neighborhood.

While we ate dinner that night, Mommy complimented Sister Gina.

"Honey, our Gina went on an errand to get cheese and also cleaned your bicycle."

Daddy looked briefly at me, and then at Sister Gina. Then, without saying anything, he just smiled.

Daddy picked up slices of cheese and put them on Sister Gina and Jade's plates. Then he startled me by putting a slice of cheese on my plate, too.

"Tonight's meal really tasted excellent."

The next day, Daddy did what he always did. He kissed Sister Gina and Jade, and then hugged Mommy. Then, he took a few steps before turning around and coming to me.

As his hand reached out toward me, my hands shot up as if through reflex to protect my face. But I didn't feel anything strike them.

Daddy carefully peeled the curtain I had made with my hands and stared at me. He then lifted me up to him and swung me around in a circle.

"You are our sweet wishing stone."

Remedial Lessons

Mommy often says to me, "Thank you for the big blessing." She says this phrase especially when she punishes me or scolds me, or when I come home very late from school.

Because I stay after school for remedial lessons, I am the last of my peers to come home. I do so long after everyone else has finished school for the day and gone home.

Mommy meets me at the front door of our house and takes my schoolbag from me. At such times, she says to me, "Thank you for the big blessing."

Schoolwork is really difficult for me.

All subjects are difficult, but math is especially difficult and painful.

Whenever I look around the class, my friends are all busy solving problems as if they all understand what is going on.

But I have no idea what is what. I am always lost. That's why I always have to go to remedial lessons.

The teacher fills the blackboard with math problems. All my friends solve the problems without any hesitation. Then they take the finished test papers up to the teacher's desk so that the teacher can grade them.

One by one, all the students go up to the teacher with their finished tests. Then, the teacher comes over to where I'm sitting. I am the only one left.

"You couldn't solve even one problem," says the teacher,

pulling at my chair and letting out a loud sigh. That one sigh is enough to freeze my feelings and stop my heart from beating.

I try hard to understand the lesson and concentrate, but the teacher's explanation is so difficult that I don't understand a thing. This experience is difficult for the teacher, too. The only thing I can do is hope that time will go by quickly. Then, when the remedial lesson is finally over, the teacher and I tidy up the chairs and desks and leave the school. My footsteps were heavy before, but heading home, my feet feel so light that I feel like I can fly.

Once I pass the stationery store outside the main school gate, I can see a small, yellow bridge up ahead. On the road leading to our neighborhood, there are paper factories, shoe factories, and brick factories here and there. The water coming out of these factories is a dark yellow and flows under the bridge. That's why my friends and I call the bridge "Yellow Bridge."

Once I cross the bridge, there is a very large paper factory. Once I pass that, there is a big onion field. With a thin sharp point at one end and a purplish space coaster at the other, it doesn't have a pleasant scent, but butterflies and bees dance and flutter about as if they were at a festival.

Next to that field, a narrow road leads to my favorite flower farm. There are metal fences all around to prevent people from cutting flowers, but in my imagination, I always reach in and cut the flowers.

Pink, red, and white. I cut the flowers, enjoy the scents, and give them to myself as encouragement. I console the empty spaces where the flowers had been. Gazing at flowers and the sun, I, who a moment ago was weak and tired, am suddenly smiling and blooming.

Energized once again, I continue past the flower farm and the brick farm. Then I see a tall poplar tree and our neighborhood, where houses are clustered about here and there.

Among the houses, our house is the one with the blue roof and the green front door. I put down my bag at the edge of the floor and head for the kitchen. From inside, Jade says to me, "Sister Silly! Wash your hands before you come in."

After washing my hands, I go back to the kitchen. Jade hands me a plate on which are two little potatoes that have cooled down.

"They were warm before," says Jade, as if she's a little bit sorry.

Even though the potatoes are cold, once I pop one into my mouth, its taste helps me forget my troubles. Two cold potatoes that have been set aside for me make me so very happy.

"You eat some, too, Jade."

She shakes her head no, but I can tell she doesn't mean that. Still, she moves her butt back. I put one potato in her hand. It's as if she's been waiting for me to do that, and she begins to eat it. This is my little sister Jade. And even though I am a bad older sister who stinks at schoolwork, I suddenly feel like a good older sister thanks to one little potato.

"Sister Silly, why do you come home so late every day?"

"Oh ..."

All of a sudden, it occurs to me that having to do remedial lessons is embarrassing.

From the next day on, during class breaks, I rush to ask my friends to explain things I don't understand. I ask and ask again.

Some friends say, "You dummy. You don't even know this." Others knock me on the head. There are even those who say, "Go away. I don't know." But I don't give up. I win them over by acting silly and continue to beg them to teach me.

Although my grades don't improve and my remedial lessons continue despite these efforts, I can feel with certainty that, somewhere in the far depths of my heart, a spark has been lit and is beginning to shine.

Books

All the bookshelves in our house are filled with books. There are so many that just looking at them annoys me. But I use them in ways that make them useful to me.

I use them as origami playing cards, chairs, pillows, blocks, insect catchers, albums for leaves and flowers, and wallets. And most commonly, I use them as tissues to wipe my snots.

I especially enjoy it when, after reading a book quickly, I tell Jade the summary. She looks at me with so much envy.

The pictures in the books add wings to my imagination.

Today is the day for story time at school. We students are supposed to go up to the front of the class and share a story with our friends.

The same few friends who always want to tell their stories raise their hands. Their stories are all similar, so it isn't that much fun.

Today's story time is particularly boring, and I become sleepy.

"Okay, anyone who wants to share an interesting story, please raise your hand."

Madeline raises her hand. Her story will undoubtedly be about a princess and a prince.

I yawn again.

Then, the teacher points at me. "Oh, Silly. Please come up and tell us your story."

While yawning, I had raised my hand without knowing it.

"Uh ... actually." While I stall and dawdle in my seat not knowing what to do, my annoying class partner, Oong Ga Ra Woon, who knows that I didn't mean to raise my hand, pokes me in the waist and urges me to stand up.

"Silly, go on up."

I'm not overcome with shivering and nervousness. Instead, I'm focused more on telling a story and getting the ordeal over with quickly. I scratch my head as I go up to the front.

What stories have I told Jade lately?

I search through the unsorted menu of stories in my head.

Was that one story called Alice the Farter?

I remember reading several books that day. In the book I remember, whenever someone farted, pot lids and houses flew high into the sky. Then there was a girl named Alice who followed a rabbit to various places.

I remember how much fun it was when I told the summary of the book to Jade.

"Silly, what is the title of the story that you'll tell your friends?" the teacher asks.

"Alice the Farter," I answer sheepishly.

"Okay, go ahead."

I'm not exactly focused. But I tell the story just as I did with Jade. Then, story time ends. From that day on, I always go up and tell a story to my class during story time.

Sweet Potato

Early one morning, we go to the field to dig up sweet potatoes.

Daddy leads the way, pulling a cart that contains hoes and shovels. Mommy has prepared several kinds of sweet breads and brought water. Sister Gina holds my hands and Jade's as we three follow behind Mommy.

At the base of the mountain a short distance outside our neighborhood, we see a small field. Down a short way from the field, a small pond is filled with green moss. Inside the pond are tadpoles, dark-striped frogs, salt fish, minnows, and other creatures. They have their own orderly system and live together.

Along the pond, there are well-groomed fields filled with corn, potatoes, pumpkins, and other edible things. Our field is different from other fields. It is in a far corner and in the shape of a dented ellipse. To get to it, we have to walk up an incline over many uneven dunes. It is on a slightly higher place than where all the flat fields are.

Various incredibly tall weeds that have shot up from the ground greet us. Theirs is an unwelcome greeting. Sweet potatoes, potatoes, beans, and peppers are growing in various spots in our field.

Daddy gets to the field a little after the rest of us. He pulls the cart over to the other side of the road and parks it under a shady tree. The first thing he does when he joins the rest of us is to let out a deep sigh. Seeing this, Mommy starts laughing and tugs on a sweet potato vine.

"Honey, the sweet potatoes turned out well."

Mommy bends down and begins pulling hard on the sweet potato stem as if she were competing in a tug-of-war. She does so with a smile on her face.

"Gina! Go with your younger sisters and pull up more stems. And make sure to tear off the leaves."

Sister Gina finds a long sweet potato stem, and then starts pulling at the stem, telling us how to do the same.

The stem is wet from having absorbed water. It makes a soft *tok tok* sound as it rests in my hand. The ground is wet and dark. Through it, we first see glimpses; then, with a pungent earthy aroma, the sweet potatoes, which are like bright jewels, gradually reveal themselves.

Beads of sweat roll off my head and land on my eyebrows. I raise my hands, which have turned dark and dirty, to wipe away the sweat, and then stare at the sky blankly.

A fleet of white clouds gathers and shows me something.

"My father is a farmer."

I rub my eyes with the back of my hand, and then stare at the sky again. The white clouds look like fresh, white, and sweet dumplings.

Mommy comes over and rubs my back.

"Silly, you must be hungry."

Ji Bong

The neighborhood corner store is filled with my favorite snacks, like orange gum and choco sandwiches.

Granny Ddee An, the storeowner, always falls asleep while she's minding the store. I think that since she sleeps like that, surrounded by tasty snacks and fruits, she must have tasty dreams. Every time the bananas that are hanging up at the front of the store shake, they gesture softly to me.

How wonderful would it be if I, too, could become the owner of a grand store like this?

Every day, I stand in front of the store's translucent glass door and imagine myself being the owner. Imagining things about a place that makes me happy just by looking at it is, in fact, one of the small parts of my daily life.

How sweetly, crisply, and softly will the gum that spreads an enticing orange scent as I chew it and the choco sandwiches that I'm holding in both my hands melt in my mouth? As I indulge myself with such fancies, Granny Ddee An, who has fallen asleep while minding the store, stretches out on the floor and sleeps comfortably.

I open the door carefully.

My bold hand picks up a pack of orange gum and hands it to myself. As I stand there, nervous and hesitant, my two feet abduct me to the hill with pine trees. As if to calm me down, my hand puts an orange gum in my mouth and my mouth begins chewing.

It feels as if the pine trees are staring at me.

The orange gum, which I thought would be so refreshing and sweet, is now just rough like a piece of thick rubber. I chew only one piece. The other four pieces go to the pine tree on which I had been leaning.

The pine tree shakes as if to say it doesn't want them, but I run off without looking back.

The next day, I'm so bothered by what happened the day before that I sit with my head on my desk throughout the class break.

My friends are filled with laughter. But my heart feels so heavy. If only I'd had money, then things wouldn't have turned out like this, I think to myself.

Crash! A friend who was running trips on a schoolbag hanging off the seat in front of me and falls to the floor.

I look closely and see that it's Sa Ba Ri, the class clown.

As I help Sa Ba Ri up off the floor, I see money in the bag

that caused the fall. I then remember that today is the day to deposit money into our school savings accounts. I continue to help Sa Ba Ri up, even as I surreptitiously slip a hand into the bag.

Sa Ba Ri returns to her seat. I rush to the bathroom. My heart beats uncontrollably fast. I feel dizzy and even start hiccupping a bit.

I hide the money inside my socks, under the soles of my feet. Then, with a shivering heart, I open the door to my classroom.

"What's going on?"

All my friends are sitting on top of their desks and receiving a punishment.

Me Ru Na Teacher is very angry. She looks at me and says, "Silly, you too. Go on top of your desk and then hold up both your arms."

As soon as she's done saying that, she begins yelling loudly.

"How can this happen in our class? The money that Jilla brought to put into her savings account is missing."

It's true. It's because of the money that I stole that all my friends are being punished.

"Before I examine all your schoolbags, I'm going to give the thief a chance to confess. Everyone, close your eyes. Whoever stole the money, put your arms down."

Sitting on the desk, I start to lower the same arms that I had just a moment ago raised.

"Silly, make sure you hold your arms straight up."

My arms shoot right back up.

"Fine. All of you are insisting that you didn't steal it. Then, there's nothing I can do."

Me Ru Na Teacher leaves the classroom, and then a little later comes right back with Gon Jal Ru No Teacher, who teaches math and is the scariest teacher.

Gon Jal Ru No Teacher's eyes are angry and wide open as he screams.

"You rascals. Put your bags on top of your knees."

Gon Jal Ru No Teacher begins inspecting not only our bags but our clothes and socks as well.

I am suddenly overwhelmed by a dark sensation. I am shivering alone at the edge of a dark cliff. I am so afraid. I don't know when it happens, but soon, tears are flowing down my cheeks.

Someone grabs my shoulders. I turn around and see that it's Me Ru Na Teacher.

"Teacher! I ..."

"Silly, put your hand down."

Me Ru Na Teacher walks back to the front of the classroom. I put my hand down and take out the money from inside my socks. Then, I stealthily slip the money into the pocket of Ji Bong's jacket, which is hanging off the chair in front of me.

In this way, Ji Bong becomes the thief who is blamed for stealing Jilla's money.

The next day, Ji Bong doesn't come to school. I hear from the other kids that Ji Bong's father came to the school.

Three days later, Ji Bong finally returns to school and quietly sits down in front of me. Ji Bong's face is covered with large, dark bruises. Ji Bong also has a limp.

No one in our class talks to Ji Bong that day.

I finally talk to Ji Bong.

"Ji Bong, are you okay?"

Ji Bong doesn't say anything. Ji Bong just leans on the desk. Like a young plant that encounters a big storm, Ji Bong is overcome with a sense of having been treated unfairly. Ji Bong is locked in shivers and tears.

Things That Can Be Seen

I like to lie down and dream whenever I have the time. The stars, the sun, and the moon all fly about inside my grasp. I always invite them into my dreams and talk with them. The time that we share together is filled with joy.

On a night filled with the chirping of crickets, Jade and I lie under the autumn sky.

"Jade! There are unusually many stars out tonight. Let's look for the brightest star."

Jade shakes her hand right above my eyes, and then sits up.

"Sister Silly, it's hazy out tonight. There are no stars. It's just dark out."

Younger Sister Jade looks at me as if I was a dummy, and then lets out a short sigh.

"You really seem dumb, just like the neighborhood people say! Why do you always say such stupid things?"

Jade is angry. She gets up and rushes away to Mommy's room.

Am I really stupid?

The stars shine so brightly, I can see them even when I close my eyes. Why can't the others see them, too?

Sure, the stars are hidden by clouds tonight. But why do people insist on seeing with their eyes to know that the stars are there. Why can't they see the stars that I can see?

When I close my eyes, all the stars fly to me.

Then, when I'm feeling excited and happy, Mommy's soft and delicate voice speaks to me.

"Gosh, I heard that you have a test tomorrow at school. But you're sleeping again?"

I don't open my eyes. Instead, I smile and say, "Mommy, I'm studying right now."

Mommy nudges me and pokes me in the rear.

"You say you're studying while sleeping. That's why your grades are lower than the ground and in the sewer."

She rustles my hair softly and then goes away.

Lying down with one's eyes closed is sleeping.

Mommy's conclusion is based exactly on what she saw.

I get up and quietly go into my room. I open a book and start reading.

"It's true. Just like Mommy and Jade said. I was sleeping."

As I sit there and try to read, the inside of my head is like some giant tangled mess of string. I can't concentrate at all. Still, Mommy must think that my sitting at my desk is commendable. She brings me a snack, compliments me for studying, and then goes away smiling.

"Persevere and sit here a little longer."

"When everyone else is sleeping, get up and dream."

My Dear Kkori

Father brought home a cute puppy from the market. I kissed its wet nose and hugged it. It then slipped like a little minnow out of my hands and began running around me with its tail wagging.

Its tail wagged about so much that it seemed as if everything around it disappeared, leaving only the puppy and me.

The puppy's tail shook so rhythmically and was so endearing that I named the puppy Kkori, which means tail.

Sometimes, when I was feeling down, all I had to do was step into the entrance of our neighborhood to smell the distinct scent of Kkori's fur. Then, Kkori would appear like a gust of wind and leap toward me. Its nose and fur would often be covered in dirt, as if it had been digging holes in the ground somewhere and rolling around in dirt.

After it was done rubbing dirt on me, it would start to lick the dirt off me as if it were sorry for getting me dirty in the first place. The dirt Kkori put on me was all focused on my face. It got to the point that it was difficult to tell who was who under the dirt.

Whenever Daddy scolded me, Kkori would console me. When I was alone without neighborhood friends, Kkori was my sole friend.

Kkori was a loyal but mischievous friend. When other kids teased and shunned me, Kkori would always go after whoever had teased me the most. Without fail, Kkori would manage to bite off that kid's shoe and parade about holding the shoe in its mouth. Kkori wouldn't even flinch when Mommy later took the shoe away and used the shoe to smack Kkori. Kkori was also good at finding things. Whenever Mommy threw the torn shoe away in the trash, Kkori would find it and put it away in its house.

One time, Mommy, who couldn't stand how Kkori was

carrying shoes about like that, waited until Kkori was gone, grabbed all the torn shoes from its house, and burned them.

Kkori was so sad and upset. Kkori didn't eat or drink for the next few days. Its nose, which was always wet and shiny, dried up. Kkori looked listless. Kkori lost weight. I got so worried that I decided to give Kkori the stuffed bear, a rare gift that Daddy had given me. To give Kkori the gift, I waited outside Kkori's house and called for Kkori. But Kkori just sat there in its house and stared listlessly at me. It didn't wag its tail even once. Kkori and I could communicate without words. I rubbed Kkori all over from its nose to its tail. Then, I gave it the stuffed bear.

━━━━━━━━━━

School was over for the day. I crossed Yellow Bridge and walked along the new road next to the onion field. The scent from the onions was particularly stinging. There was no wind, but the onion plants were dancing anyway. Onion seeds flew up, formed a white cluster, and then raced toward me. I rubbed my eyes with my hands. When I lowered my hands, I smelled Kkori. Kkori was waiting for me today, even way out here in the onion field.

But our happiness was fleeting. I looked over at the ruined patch of the onion field that KKori had just trampled. We had to get out of there right away or else we'd get in trouble. We ran home so fast that our breathing was heavy and the inside of my mouth felt dry.

Kkori filled up the house with the smell of onions.

"This is not good. Kkori, come here."

I worked hard to pump up water and gave Kkori a bath. Still, I couldn't remove the little bits and pieces of the onion plant that remained stuck to its fur. Kkori decided to help me and shook itself off vigorously until the bits and pieces of the onion plant finally fell off.

I showered Kkori off with water and dried its fur. Somehow,

the onion scent was still there. It suddenly occurred to me to try Mommy's perfume. I went into Mommy's room and rubbed pink perfume powder on Kkori. Kkori coughed a bit, and then endearingly wagged its tail. The pink perfume powder got rubbed in thoroughly through its fur. Then, Kkori shook itself and sent some of the powder back to me.

Before we knew it, Kkori regained the weight it had lost. But, like me, Kkori had a big appetite. I worried that it might eat too much. Still, I was so very proud of Kkori, who had become strong again.

Around dawn one morning, an unfamiliar screaming woke our family from sleep. A strange man with a dark face was crouched on the floor, cowering before Kkori. The next morning, Kkori was treated to a feast. Then, a few days later, Daddy built Kkori a brand new house with a blue roof. It was bigger and cleaner than Kkori's old one. Inside the new house were old shoes that Mommy had thought to place there, along with my stuffed bear.

Energized and invigorated, Kkori wagged its tail all day long that day.

The next morning, Kkori yawned a lot and sat still with its eyes open. What was wrong? Kkori had eaten the food mixed with rat poison that we'd laid out to kill rats. Mommy had been worried that exactly such a thing might happen, so she'd wrapped the poison-laced food with string. We don't know if the string came undone on its own or if Kkori undid the string, but Kkori, who had such a strong appetite, ate the rat poison. My sole friend was gone.

Our family drowned in sadness without Kkori. I was so angry and upset that Kkori had left me. I tried to suppress these feelings that hurt me so much. But even as I tried to suppress these feelings, they only grew bigger. The joyful laughter of the freshly bloomed flowers of the onion plants, the nodding of heads from clusters of trees, and the winks from stars at night could not console me.

Every day, I just sat quietly in front of Kkori's house and cried. And I grumbled to Kkori, the mean dog that had left me.

"What are we to do with the old shoes, the stuffed bear, and the new dog house that Daddy built for you? You left behind your body, you spiteful thing. You left behind too many memories for my dumb brain to remember. You left by yourself. I've inherited all your things. They're so heavy—it hurts too much!"

Little Kkori

After Kkori left us, I was overwhelmed by the fact that I couldn't see Kkori even if I wanted to. Each night, I cried under the covers, missing Kkori. I don't even know how much I cried, because I felt so alone without Kkori.

Through the window, I saw a single cloud, a boulder, and a tree standing alone by themselves. The cloud, boulder, and tree all seemed to be suffering with me. We all seemed unable to forget the memory of Kkori. I was locked away in my sadness. Naturally, all things around me also were similarly locked in sadness.

Drawing up courage, I opened the window and laughed loudly. When I did that, my laughter struck the cloud, the boulder, and the tree. These things sent me a bright smile. My heart felt lighter.

But I found out that night just how fleeting my sadness and loneliness really were; they were not at all as light as I thought at that moment. I had finished my homework and was lingering in the yard. Mommy came home from the market with a large cardboard box. Through the holes that had been cut out on top of the box, I heard a familiar sound.

"Silly, go ahead and open it."

I started to do so and glimpsed two clear, glistening jewels.

"What is this, Mommy?"

As soon as I opened the box, something bounced up and licked my face. It was a small puppy!

Still, I reacted as if nothing in the world could ever replace my precious Kkori. I ignored the new puppy and went into my room.

A little later, Sister Gina and Jade fawned over how cute the new puppy was and hugged it. The puppy lashed out against them and stumbled about. It wanted only me.

Through the window, I could again see the cloud, the boulder, and the sole tree. Inside Kkori's house, a white light was on.

It's Kkori!

I went over and sat down in front of Kkori's house.

Little Kkori wagged its tail and came toward me. It couldn't wag its tail quite as vigorously as Kkori had back then, but it still began to tame and insert itself in my heart. Every time Little Kkori wagged its tail, it made all the beautiful memories of Kkori a bit dimmer. But before I knew it, every day after that, Little Kkori and I began building a new memory together.

"You are Little Kkori. Let's get along well together."

Watching Little Kkori in front of dear Kkori's house, I finally started to say a long-overdue farewell.

"At first, I was so sad and it hurt so much that it felt like I was going to die. I tried to do something, but whatever I tried only made me sadder. Then, in the end, when I stopped trying, a new happiness came into my life. It's as if you, my dear Kkori, have sent me a gift. Good-bye, my dear Kkori."

Sabrina

I finally had a friend who was my age in my neighborhood. Her name was Sabrina. She was tall, pretty, and had long shiny hair. She really looked like a princess.

This Sabrina wanted so much to meet me that she moved to our neighborhood on a stormy day filled with fierce winds, thunder, and heavy rains. According to Sister Gina, Mommy and Granny Ho Ya helped them move in.

Once Sabrina moved in, Hingee, who lived in Granny Ho Ya's home, had nothing to do anymore and just lingered about. Finally, Hingee was sold to the market. Hingee, who had crowed every morning, had lost its job to Sabrina. But Sabrina woke up the entire neighborhood in a rather sad way by clinging to her mother, crying, and begging her not to go to work.

Every time Sabrina cried like that, I covered my ears, sat in a corner, and shivered with unease. And every time I did that, Mommy hugged me and sang me a song.

One quiet day when there was no sound of Sabrina crying, a woman with red nails brought Sabrina to our house. The woman was Sabrina's mother. She smelled of cigarettes and other unpleasant things. She also frowned a lot, but she was still very pretty. I couldn't help but think that Sabrina was pretty because she'd taken after her mother.

My mother is also pretty, but why don't I look pretty? I fretted for a moment.

After that day, Sabrina stood outside our house every morning and called for me. She always had her schoolbag on, and her pockets were filled with money for cookies and candy. Walking to school with pretty Sabrina, I showed her the hill filled with pine trees and all my other little friends along the way.

We got together often in school and played in the schoolyard. Sometimes, she brought friends with her to my classroom and teased me for being dumb, but I didn't mind this.

After one semester like that, Sabrina, who'd show up outside our house each morning, suddenly stopped coming.

So I went to her house and called for her to go to school together. She dodged my request.

"You go ahead, Silly."

I wanted to play with her, so I went over to her house with my dolls. But she wouldn't see me.

"Silly, playing with you is no fun. I don't want to play with you."

Sabrina spoke coldly. Her words sapped me of strength and upset me. But it was okay, because all around me, I had friends who were always there for me.

Then one Sunday, when the unpleasant memory of Sabrina had almost faded away, it began raining fiercely from early morning. There was thunder and lightning. Sabrina's mother was nowhere to be seen. But an old woman, who looked a lot like Sabrina's mother, and Sabrina, who was for a short time a good friend to me, moved away. They did so in such terrible weather as if they were running away from something. Sabrina's hair was a mess. Biting her nails, red like her mother's, as if she was nervous, she disappeared in the distance.

Ice Cream

Loyola is the smartest student in my class and grade. She is the darling of all the teachers and the most popular student. I am proud to say that this popular Loyola became my friend.

Loyola is too busy to play with me at school, but often comes to our village with her real-estate developer father and plays with me then.

After eating a grand weekend lunch, I'm about to go for a walk with Little Kkori, when Loyola's voice calls to me from outside our front door.

"Silly, are you there?"

"Loyola! Just a minute. I'll be right out."

I'm so happy she's there that I rush out without even putting on my shoes all the way.

"You came with your dad again?"

"Yeah, I came with Dad and two of his employees."

"I see. Loyola, let's go play in the forest where there are acorn trees."

When we get to the acorn trees in the forest, we startle squirrels that are gathering acorns from the ground. The squirrels scurry back up the trees and flee.

Loyola and I make crowns and skirts with leaves and tree branches. We play make-believe princess and make-believe house.

Sitting on a tree stump, Loyola calls to me.

"Hey, Silly! I heard something from my dad. It's a secret. If you promise not to tell anyone, I will tell you. Can you promise to keep a secret?"

"I promise."

"Okay. Do you know Jjam Bul Long Town?"

"Jjam Bul Long?"

"You know. That place where we went on our school field trip last fall."

"Our school field trip last fall. I remember now. That's the place with a lot of apple trees."

"Right. That's Jjam Bul Long Town. A large factory moved in to that town. Do you know what kind of factory it is?"

"No, I don't know."

Loyola looks around to make sure no one else can hear. Then she puts her mouth to my ear and whispers in a low voice.

"It's an ice cream factory."

"An ice cream factory?"

"Yes. And don't faint when I tell you the next part. They have so much ice cream there that at noon, they give out free ice cream to people who line up. My dad brought home a whole bunch of free ice cream from there some time ago."

What Loyola has just told me is shocking and exciting. I do nearly faint from hearing it.

"Silly, remember that this is a secret that I'm telling only you. As I said before, you can't tell anyone else. My dad told me not to tell anyone."

I nod. I am determined to keep her secret. Then we put our pinkies together to seal the promise.

Holding such a huge and important secret, I part with Loyola and come home.

Day and night, I am so engrossed in thoughts about the ice cream factory that I lose my appetite, my eyes grow dazed, and I begin to look like someone who is sick.

This coming weekend, I'm going to go to the ice cream factory. I'll get a whole bunch of ice cream, and then our family can eat ice cream until we're nearly bursting, I think to myself.

Then I rush to the kitchen and ask Mommy for the biggest plastic bag we have. Mommy asks me what I need it for, but I just keep insisting I need it and throwing a tantrum.

Mommy looks all over, and then finally hands me a large plastic bag.

The weekend finally comes. I am so excited that I don't sleep a wink the night before. I sit inside the kitchen and wait for Mommy. Early in the morning, Mommy comes into the kitchen with her apron on. Seeing a figure crouching there in the dark, she is frightened and lets out a scream. Her scream wakes the rest of the family. Mommy realizes it's me and asks me what I am doing there.

"Please hurry and give me breakfast."

Daddy, who comes over to see what is going on, returns to his room with a blank expression. Sister Gina begins teasing me.

"I should have known. Your appetite has finally returned to you."

Because of me, our family has a very early breakfast.

As soon as I am done eating, I hold the large plastic bag close to my chest and speak.

"Mommy, my teacher told us to go out and pick up litter for homework. I'll come back after I'm done with this assignment."

My family all stare at me as if in disbelief. Then Mommy goes into the kitchen and returns with a smaller plastic bag.

"Silly, leave that plastic bag here. Take this one instead."

I clutch the large plastic bag that I have and rush out of the house.

Sister Gina's voice trails after me.

"Hey, do you plan to pick up every piece of trash in our neighborhood with such a large plastic bag? Gosh, you're an idiot."

Even though it is early, there are many cars and people out. It will be a while before it is noon, so I calm myself and start walking slowly. Perhaps it is because I am walking slowly and not in a rush, but things that I didn't notice before suddenly seem dangerous.

Cars that should have heeded red lights just race through them at frighteningly fast speeds. People also rush about and cross streets in a dangerous manner.

I wait at the crosswalk for the light to change. From across the street, a man looks about and then starts crossing against the light. He doesn't see a car that is racing right at him. The car collides with him. People gather about. I can hear the siren of a police car.

At that moment, as I watch all these people in front of me, I feel as if I am a creature of leisure. I continued past the site of the car accident. Even though I continue to walk slowly and unhurriedly, I get to the town early.

There are many apple trees in the town. From the entrance to the town, the refreshing scent of apples makes me feel good. For some reason, the apples that hang in clusters here and there seem empty and lonely.

After passing the apple orchard, I see a gray factory with a large chimney at the base of a mountain that has been stripped of trees. I don't know why, but my footsteps become heavy and force me to stop. All of a sudden, I don't want to go there anymore. So I encourage myself.

I startled my family so early this morning. How good would it be if I returned to them with a whole bunch of ice cream?

With that thought, I urge myself to keep going.

Finally, I reach the metal front gate of the factory, but there is no one else who has come for the free ice cream.

There's no one else here. Does that mean I have to take all the ice cream that they're giving out?

I begin to worry like that. I become nervous and wait for a long while, opening and folding my large plastic bag.

Finally, a small door on a small panel of the large front gate creaks open. A very thin and shabby-looking man who smells awful steps out. He walks past me for a bit, and then comes back to me.

He then says, "Who are you?"

"I am Silly."

"What are you doing here? Who are you looking for?"

"What do you mean, who am I looking for? I'm here for the free ice cream."

"What? Who told you that they're going to buy you ice cream?"

"Not buy. I know that this factory gives out free ice cream to people at noon."

"What? You look kind of silly, and it looks like someone told you a silly lie."

"No, that can't be. It's not a lie."

"Listen, little kid. This isn't an ice cream factory. This is a leather factory."

"A leather factory? Then is there any other factory around here?"

"This is the only factory in this town. So stop talking nonsense and hurry back home."

I just stand there in a daze with my empty plastic bag. The man speaks again.

"Little kid, if you want to eat ice cream so badly, then go and ask your father to buy you some."

I stare blankly at the man until he finally disappears back into the factory. Then I turn around.

The plastic bag that holds no ice cream flutters in the wind. My heart also flutters about as if frightened and makes strange noises.

I am back at the apple orchard. I console my sadness with tears colored by the reddish gleam of the apples all around me.

Breathing

Although it is the middle of the day, it suddenly turns dark as if it were night and thick raindrops begin to fall. Trees that had been dry refresh themselves with a wash.

I stare at the window, and then quietly look around the room. What is this soft sound I hear in my room, a sound that seems as if it is where the current has stopped flowing? This distinct sound grows ever louder as I focus on it.

I focus all my senses to locate that sound. It draws increasingly closer to me. But before I find its source, I first find my belly, which moves up and down. The breath that I draw in and spit out is never ending. I hold my breath for a bit, and my belly stops moving. I hold my breath even longer, and my entire body shakes wildly before the breath bursts out of me and I'm forced to take another breath.

The sun slides through the window. I open the window and see that the rain has stopped. I can see a tiny something crawling down slowly from the window. It's an ant. I try to touch it with a pencil that had been rolling on the floor. The ant crawls up and away.

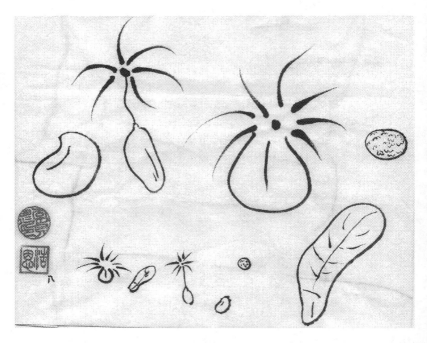

I hear something from the shed.

Daddy goes up a ladder to the roof of the shed and then comes back down.

Belly goes up and down.

In and out.

Breathing in. Breathing out.

A hand closes and then opens.

Eyes close and then open.

Mouth closes and then opens.

Breathing is such a simple thing, but I have been thinking of it as something so serious and complex.

Mommy calls for me and says it's time for dinner. But I'm not hungry. Something has made me forget my wish to eat so that I don't even feel hungry. Whatever it is, it's interesting and fun.

Breathe in and out.

Breathe out and in. This keeps repeating.

A graph that I don't understand fills my head as I experience these realizations. I eventually figure out what it is.

Pumpkin

The whole village is filled with excitement over the annual Vine Festival. Our village is a farming village, so to share the joy of the harvest, we select the biggest and prettiest of the produce that grows on vines. There aren't any large prizes or any prize money, but it's still an important festival that everyone in the village enjoys together.

Our family only farms a small plot, but each year, we enter our sweet potatoes in the competition. Even though our sweet potatoes never have finished in the top three, everyone in the village praises our sweet potatoes for being the tastiest.

The reason I so eagerly await the festival is that Granny Ho Ya, our next-door neighbor, nearly always wins first place with her large pumpkin.

Granny Ho Ya's pumpkin will undoubtedly take first place again this year.

Before the start of the festival, I see Granny Hoya carefully clean her pumpkin in her storeroom. The pumpkin she had last year was huge, but her pumpkin this year is gigantic.

The day before the festival, we watch as Mommy and Daddy attach the cart to our bicycle. Mommy holds the sweet potatoes that she's wrapped carefully and sits inside the cart. Then we three sisters get on behind her.

We submit our king-sized sweet potatoes to the festival committee and then decorate the official spot where we're to display them. While Mommy and Daddy put on the finishing touches on the decorating, we three sisters go around and admire the other vegetables one more time before the contest officially starts the next day.

They are things that we are familiar with and often eat, but the vegetables in the contest seem to be completely different. They are so big, and their colors are so vibrant and glamorous. They seem not to be things to be eaten, but rather food items that are to be admired. We continue looking around and being amazed. Granny Ho Ya's pumpkin hasn't arrived yet.

Last year's winner doesn't have to go through the same submission process. Instead, last year's winner automatically gets to display at a special spot right in the front. But Granny Ho Ya's pumpkin isn't there. There's only an empty spot where it should be.

We stay at the festival grounds for a long time, eating tasty things and seeing the sights before the actual start of the festival. But, in the back of our heads, we are all worried and waiting for Granny Ho Ya. Mommy and Daddy seem to be worrying, too.

Then, while the festival preparation continues, Daddy brings the bicycle over, puts us in the cart, and ferries us back home. Thinking about the festival that will take place the next day, I'm so excited I can't fall asleep. For just such times, I've found a way to bring about sleep. All I have to do is stare at the sky.

I stare out the window at the sky. It looks like tomorrow will be a clear day. The moon is bright, and the stars are sparkling. Late that night, I see Mommy and Daddy come out of Granny Ho Ya's house. Daddy has a serious expression on his face. He says something to Mommy.

What's going on?

It's tough enough falling asleep tonight that I'm already busy staring at the sky. But seeing Mommy and Daddy like that chases all sleep from me. Mommy and Daddy go to bed soon after that.

How much time passes?

Staring obstinately at the sky, my eyes slowly close. Just then, a bright light comes on inside Granny Ho Ya's storeroom.

I can't be patient any longer. I don't want to wake my family up, so I carefully step outside. It's early in the morning. Walking barefoot on the dirt feels like I'm walking on a road made of soft cotton. The door of Granny Hoya's storeroom is open a crack. I quietly peer inside. Granny Ho Ya is sitting in front of a huge pumpkin.

I call for her cautiously.

"Granny Ho Ya."

It seems she doesn't hear me. I go over and sit on the same pile of hay that she's sitting on. She turns to me slowly and then gulps loudly when she sees me.

"Silly, why are you up at this time of the day?"

"Granny, you aren't sleeping either."

"Ahh, you little thing. Hurry back, and go to sleep. Granny will go in and sleep, too."

"Yes, Granny. But why is this pumpkin still here?"

"Are you curious?"

Instead of an answer, I stare blankly at her.

"Let's see. I'm not really sure what I'm doing."

Granny Ho Ya seems hesitant. She then speaks again.

"Silly, I really like you. You always laugh as if you're happy."

Granny speaks sheepishly and then smiles.

"That's why when I see you, I can't help but smile. You're small and young. But you make me feel comfortable. I can sense that you are solid inside and healthy. That's why I like you so much."

I am confused. She started out talking about her pumpkin, but then has veered off for some reason to tell me why she likes me.

I don't even remember to thank her for her compliment. I am so curious about her pumpkin that I ask again.

"What about your pumpkin, Granny?"

"Right. The pumpkin. I think this pumpkin is like Granny's greed. On the outside, it looks magnificent and good. To grow a truly magnificent pumpkin requires many times the care, attention, and concern required to grow an ordinary one."

Granny stares right at me.

"Silly, do you think this pumpkin looks good?"

She touches the pumpkin and rubs it.

"Yes, Granny. It's terrific."

Granny taps the pumpkin and laughs.

"This pumpkin isn't a real pumpkin. If you want to eat it and try to cut it with a knife, it will only disappoint you. It's all empty inside. It lacks true taste and will go bad too quickly. But the funny thing is, while I paid so much attention to this pumpkin, all the other small and big pumpkins never complained to me. They grew well on their own and made me happy. Those other pumpkins are solid inside. They don't trouble me. They grew well on their own and only help me."

Granny lifts me and sits me on her lap.

"That's why I started thinking after I picked this big pumpkin. While I was absorbed in my own greed and focused only on this one pumpkin, those other pumpkins grew by themselves and now give me joy and strength. I now feel so sorry to these other pumpkins. That's why I've decided to stop working on making big pumpkins that only grow out of my greed."

"Then, what will you do with this terrific pumpkin?"

"Silly, what would you like me to do with it?"

"It's Granny's pumpkin."

"Yes, you're right. I know what to do."

Granny then gets up.

It is the day of the festival. I wake up filled with a fragrant and refreshing sensation. I then lie inside the cart attached to Daddy's bicycle.

I get out of the cart and go to the spot where our king-sized sweet potatoes are on display. In the distance, I see Granny Ho Ya and Mommy standing where Granny Ho Ya's display is. They are surrounded by a crowd of people. Granny Ho Ya and Mommy both have aprons on and are handing out pumpkin pies to people. And on the large display basket in front of them, there are many healthy but small pumpkins.

Lips

A rustling wakes me from sleep. Auntie and Mommy have their heads together and are deep in conversation.

"Auntie."

"Wow, Silly finally woke up."

Mommy comes over to me. She takes my sweat-soaked shirt off and helps me change into a new shirt.

"Here, these are for you."

Auntie hands me a gift set in the shape of a boot. The boot is filled with cookies and candy.

Auntie is visiting us for the first time in a long while. She has a lot to talk about with Mommy. After she gives me the gift, she goes right back to talking to Mommy.

I stare at Auntie.

Her lips are unusually red and bright. Every time they move, it seems as if a red cherry is shaking. Auntie sees me staring at her and laughs out loud.

"You must be very bored. What do you want to do with Auntie?"

"Auntie, let's go outside."

"Okay, Silly. Shall we take a walk around the village?"

Instead of an answer, I rush and put on my shoes.

Auntie asks Mommy where Sister Gina and Jade are.

Mom answers as she goes into the kitchen.

"They went outside with the gift set you gave them. They're probably at the playground out front."

Auntie, who's putting on her slippers, makes a request to Mommy.

"Sis, I want to eat noodles."

From the kitchen, Mommy's voice flows out.

"Sure. Take your time going there and coming back."

Auntie and I walk around the village.

Maybe it is uncomfortable for Auntie to walk with me because my stride is so short. Whatever the reason, at one point, she puts me on her back and carries me as we continue around the village. Before she got her present job, Auntie lived with us for a short while. That's why the villagers know her. They greet her, and she greets them back. Every time she does so, I stare at her shiny, pretty lips.

Interestingly, I notice that Auntie bites her lips when she talks with people and licks her lips when she is done talking. She keeps doing this. I stare at her lips even more closely. Shockingly, they seem to get prettier, redder, and shinier.

Auntie stays with us for two days and then leaves on Friday. Then, on Sunday, after we eat breakfast, Mommy diligently finishes doing the dishes and other housework before she comes out to the yard, holding a metal bucket, and calls Sister Gina, Jade and me.

"Come on, kids. Let's go pick some cherries."

In front of our house, there is a small field that has some lilacs and two cherry trees. I haven't paid much attention to this cherry tree, which is much bigger than I am. So naturally, I did not know that its cherries are ripe.

Spurred on by Mommy's suggestion, I look at the cherry tree. It's filled with red cherries.

Mommy and Sister Gina pick cherries. I stretch my arms as far as they can go and manage to pick a few pinkish cherries. Jade eats cherries and spits out the seeds. Seeing all those cherries, I recall Auntie's shiny red lips.

All of a sudden, an idea comes to me. Maybe if I do what Auntie does with her lips, then I too can have pretty lips like hers. So I bite my lips and then lick them.

There aren't that many cherries in our basket, but we wash them in water. Then after setting aside a portion for Daddy, the rest of us sit with Mommy and eat them. The cherries are sour and not that sweet. But I think that eating them will help me get red lips, so I force myself to eat them.

"Silly really eats cherries well. That's probably why her lips are like cherries."

That one praise from Mommy makes Sister Gina and Jade stare at my lips.

I quickly bite my lips and then lick them.

Jade tugs at Mommy's sleeve and speaks.

"Mommy, Sister Silly's lips are red and shiny."

Mommy puts the rest of the remaining cherries in her mouth and says, "You're right. They really are like that."

This is it. My lips are really turning pretty like Auntie's lips.

I spend the rest of the day determined to make my lips prettier.

Monday morning, a strange noise wakes me up.

Daddy's face, Mommy's face, Sister Gina's face, and Jade's face are hovering right above me. They are staring right at me.

Then Sister Jade says, "Mommy, Daddy, why are Silly's lips like that?"

Confused, I drag myself up. Sister Gina rushes over to me with a mirror that was hanging on the wall. She shines the mirror on me.

My lips are swollen. They are so swollen that they look like they cover nearly half my face. They have become catfish lips.

Bread

On payday, Daddy always comes home with a large bag filled with corn bread. To prevent us sisters from fighting over the bread, Mommy divides the bread into equal parts and hands them out to us.

I like to eat, so as soon as I get the bread from Mommy, it goes right inside my mouth. To make the bread taste even better, I imagine that its rough texture is soft. I also imagine all sorts of other tastes to enhance the bread's taste.

It's sad, but the bread doesn't last long. Soon, only a small morsel the size of a cotton ball is left. At that time, I give the morsel to Little Kkori, who has been waiting during the whole time, wagging its tail and watching me enjoy my food.

Little Kkori devours the bread in one bite and then stares at me as if it wished there were more. I take Little Kkori for a walk around the village.

Eating is joyous. Eating the bread that Daddy buys for us makes us incomparably happy.

Early the next morning, Little Kkori and I return from a walk to the hill with pine trees. Jade is sitting there crying. The rest of the family stares daggers at me. Mommy is frowning and walks away. Daddy looks angry. He stares at me for a while, and comes over to me. Then he slaps my cheek hard.

"You're like a stupid parasite. After eating so much, you still haven't had enough. So you go and steal your little sister's share."

I am confused. I've been slapped, but I don't know why. I stare at Daddy.

"You think staring at me with that confused look is going to make me forgive you, you sick girl?"

Daddy then picks up a broom and starts hitting me with it.

My body hurts. From my head to my toes, my whole body feels like someone is holding a fire to it. It hurts and stings.

Strangely enough, I keep seeing Ji Bong's face. I think

about saying something, but change my mind. Something warm rubs my face. I touch it with my hand. It's blood.

Mommy rushes out of her room, grabs Daddy's hands, and tries to stop him.

"If you keep this up, you'll kill the child."

Daddy throws the broom on the ground as if he were waiting for someone to stop him, and then he storms out of the house.

"Jade put her share of the bread aside to eat later. Now that bread is gone."

Daddy thinks that because I like to eat so much, I must be the thief who stole Jade's bread.

I had been awakened early that morning because of a strange rustling sound. I had seen Sister Gina eating something. That must have been Jade's bread.

My stupid unbearable smile appears again on my face.

Ji Bong, about what happened to you that time—can we now call it even? I'm really sorry. Please forgive me.

I want to ask for Ji Bong's forgiveness, but lacking courage, all I can do is silently say I am sorry inside my heart. I keep hearing Mommy's voice in fits and spurts. I am shaking.

"Silly, wake up. Wake up."

Listlessly, I am sucked away somewhere in a swirl. From a distance, Sister Gina stares at me blankly.

Chapter 3: Inside Myself

The swirl that sucked me inside was a tunnel that was so bright that I couldn't open my eyes. I tried to open my eyes with all my strength but couldn't do so. Only by cringing and squinting could I see barely see anything.

I was in a space filled with white lights. The place was so quiet that my ears grew dull. A tiny tadpole-like thing came to me and whispered:

"Is there no sound?"

"Is there no color?"

"Is there no smell?"

"Is there no sensation?"

"They are all lies."

The murmurs came from here and there. Their yapping made my head feel as if it were about to burst open.

"What are you talking about?"

The question that I had spoken aloud bounced about like an echo. Many lights rushed over to me. They lifted me and threw me down.

My body bounced about. I couldn't escape from the mental daze.

I felt a strange sensation. Something large or small pushed

and pulled me. And a small pulling force had me firmly in its grasp.

"Do not be afraid. Trust me, and rest your body with me. We must ride well the stream that cannot be seen. This place is dangerous. They are changing very fast. It's not clear where the seismic center is, but the toxins are spreading."

I was afraid and asked in a whimpering voice, "Who are you?"

After hesitating slightly, the small pulling force spoke again.

"The Great Silly will find that out in good time. In the meantime, let us go."

This thing knows who I am.

For a brief instant, I got on and rode the stream that couldn't be seen. And then for a short time, I met sunlight there.

It was a truly welcome meeting.

However, sunlight did not shower me with warmth and comfort. It was cold and serious. It was not the sunlight, the kiddy lamp, which I remembered from my past. It was cold and heartless. Its treatment of me was stinging and painful. I was very startled.

Father's words came to mind.

"Sunlight is a blessing, for which we are grateful. Living and being able to see the sun adds joy to our days."

Thus, I briefly met cold sunlight. Then the certain stream that could not be seen pulled me to another place.

My body was hot as if it were a ball of flame. My body stung so much that I could not bear it.

"It will shake a lot. If it pushes, Master Silly, focus your strength on the lower part."

I tried with all my human strength to find a stream that contained some sensation. Various streams that could not be seen flowed all about me. I focused my strength on my lower parts and floated down along one such stream.

The stream traveled so fast that I felt nauseous and shook

a lot. I slipped through an opening that was cold, thick, and white. I entered a remote and isolated place.

This time, I had come upon a place that was extremely slow.

I saw a large transparent giant, who was tearing at his white flesh and crying, *"Oooh, ooh, oong, jjuhk."*

When I reached my hand out to touch the giant, his cries erupted into a waterfall.

This was the water of life, that precious and mysterious entity about which Father had spoken. I thought back to the time when we had seen a dried-up grape tree. Father had said that water was hope. This place was the realm of water. Hope lived here.

"A tree, whatever may be the case, has hope. Even when it is fallen, it can sprout again and grow again. Even when its roots grow old in the soil, even when parts of it die buried underground, as long as it tastes water, it can grow again as if it were a young sapling."

But this water of life refuses to flow and remains stagnant.

Everything is scary.

The water remained unmoving. I feared that it was changing in a strange way because of them.

This is an emergency! If water does not do what it should, it will surely become cursed. And this curse will spread to all those things and all people who depend on water.

My heart had grown anxious. Still, I consoled the water. Then holding it close to me, I threw myself outside. Water, which had been introverted and still, began to run wildly as soon as we were outside. Water began to wet and bless all those things of nature that needed its blessing. As I traveled about, all the while embracing water close to my heart, a kind rock whispered to me.

"Water is the most delicious thing in this world."

I continued to hug water and traveled with it all about.

However, water slowly started to act mean and began to be increasingly more capricious. It was calm, and then it would suddenly shake violently and swirl about. It would be peaceful, and then suddenly explode lashing out here and there. It truly had countless faces.

Then, as we moved along a low path, I spotted a stream of water that seeped into the ground. I followed this stream of water into the ground.

Underground, it was eerily hot and strange cries of pain echoed all about.

"Are you hurting?"

A person I could barely make out was shivering as if he were indescribably cold. He was tearing his own flesh and in great pain.

Seeing him thus, I also felt pain.

That person hadn't been blessed with the others; however, he had been cursed with them. He had held them. And, because they would surely return to him, their curse was also his curse.

I continued deeper into the ground. There, I began to see the pillars that Father had placed there. A few were damaged, but most of them had been placed well and stood firmly.

Father had sympathized with the beautiful man, who was

now shivering in the cold, and had quietly placed these pillars of life there without anyone's knowledge.

"Where are the pillars that hold up the ground? I have placed strong pillars to hold up the ground."

The beautiful one, whom they did not know, had strong pillars placed within. However, no matter how strong these pillars were, if their greed drilled holes in them and made them shake, there could be no curse greater than this.

They were pillars set in place by Father, but their greed and hubris made me fear still.

"Oh, Ye Great One! I have seen the boiling wrath that you, in all your beauty and generosity, have hidden away."

Blank Space

Within his space, there are spaces that cannot be filled.
Even though they appear not to be filled, I hope that you will
not try to upturn or fill them.
All the sensations that come from feeling and seeing are lies.
I hope that you will leave the space that contains reason as it
is ...

In your space, there is a gap that cannot be filled.
Even though this appears not to be filled, I hope that you
will not try to poke at it or fill it. All the sensations that
come from feeling and hearing are lies.
I hope that you will leave the gap that contains reason as it
is ...

That blank space is the last remaining refuge of a deferred
life.

Maturation

Do not hate or shun your suffering.
Do not hate or shun your sadness.
Do not hate or shun your pain.
Do not hate or shun your despair.
Do not hate or shun your hardship.
Do not hate or shun your fear.
Do not hate or shun your loneliness.
Do not hate or shun your wounds.
When they take root as part of that which is precious to
    you,
All these things will shine brightly within you.
Then you will be born anew.

Dot

Always suffering from nightmares
Always losing sleep
Always anxious
For me, who suffers so, Father sat at my bedside and
consoled.

Do you know what love is?
Do you know what suffering is?
Do you know what joy is?
Do you know what sadness is?
They are all a single dot.

Advance Notice

Passing a winding road, I enter a small, wooden cabin.
The place feels familiar.
Inside the open door, another door leads to the backyard.
I go around a low partition and find myself in a familiar
place.
Another door opens, leading to yet another backyard.
Once again, I go around the low partition.
I open doors again and again, only to encounter yet another
partition. Slowly, terror pushes into me and makes me run
and run.
Out of breath and anxious, I crouch, cover my ears, and
shiver.
One of my ears itches; a round piece of earwax crawls out.
From my other ear, my hand catches something again.
Tissues from inside an ear? I yank on the tissue, and it slides
out, seemingly without end.
It's as if my ear has been blocked all this time. The tissue
keeps coming out. I want it to end, and it finally ends.
My body shivers so much, it's difficult to stand. I try to
clear my head by shutting and opening my eyes.
Right in front of me, I see a hole for dogs.
I crawl through the hole as if escaping from something and
come out into a backyard.
I lift my head and stand up. Dark spirits, holding sticks,
gather from everywhere.
Not knowing where to go, I take a step back and fall into a
sea.
A group of whales who appear from somewhere gather and
swim around me as if they want me to see something.
It's as if they're imploring me to witness their agony.

The whales dance about in painstaking movements, which I cannot ignore.

All the whales have been cut and scratched up all over.

They cry from the pain of these wounds.

The sea in which these whales dance is withered and poor.

In that poor sea, the whales stop dancing and point at yet another sea.

Underneath that second sea, something resembles you.

Its back is pierced with so many sharp metal needles, and it hasn't eaten or even found much food.

This monster can't cry out, even though it is in great pain.

A few of the whales use their fins to strike at and pass food to the monster that resembles you.

Touched by this sight, I yell out.

"Mutation!"

The whales immediately look about, surround me, and then cover my mouth.

"Keep quiet. He must not hear that."

The whales that surrounded me move aside. A white whale appears and stares at me.

"I went up to where they lived and told them through my death, but they did not understand."

Soul

I suffered extremely sad pain from someone.
I experienced increasing suffering from something.
I met intense loneliness from that thing.

Each one causing pain and suffering wanted to be
connected to the other through a link, and so, through
earnest desire, each rushed at the other with tenacity.
But, this was not enough. Day and night, the desire took
me around to all places.
Once I became a disgrace. Everyone said I was dirty, and so
they all showered me with spit, kicks, and curses.
This unbearable hardship repeated itself, and I had to
endure it and persevere.

Everything inside me shook and jumped about in madness.
When I met myself for the first time, I sprang up and tried
to burst through, shouting, "I will destroy everyone!"
This happened countless times, and each time, I held
myself and prayed.
*Please lower me to a more lowly place. Please put me to
sleep peacefully.*

Finally, the link that tried so hard to connect rusted on its
own and disappeared.
That which was so hard to endure melted away on its own
into nothingness.

Whether you are big or small, be vigilant of the self who is
proud of its power.
Be vigilant of all those who brag of their marvelous power.

How fleeting and meaningless is power, which is less significant than an insect that lives for just a day or a grain of dust.
I hope that this power is allowed to rest and cultivate in that space, which is both small and large, within me.

Emptying

The moment you took the forbidden fruit and bit into it, you knew the door to thoughts had been opened.

You want to have certain things. You want to do certain things. You want to know certain things.

No matter what you have, you wish to add to it. You begin to desire and to despair desperately.

That which we launched without design now approaches to remove the curtains that hide.

A force that is foreign to instinct pulls all things through you down the path of self-destruction.

The time to restore things to the way they were has passed, but if you want to forge a changed path, then cast those things aside.

There is no way to know whether your heart and those things will stop, but do not be tied to silly longing. Simply empty it.

Don't be a slave to instinct that strives greedily only to grow filled. Instead, start emptying to lighten your thoughts and hearts.

Self

"These things I give unto you. Own them, and take care of them well."

Your caretaking is always shaky and precarious, like walking a tightrope.
In an instant, caretaking turns into disaster, and then what results?
You have become a hostage to twisted thinking and a twisted heart.
Eyes become mouth. Ears become anus. Everything becomes a mess.
How dare you think so carelessly and open your hearts so carelessly!
You locked up a living spirit with so little care and refused to release that spirit.
You changed the meaning of *being* to your own meaning, and then served and followed it.
You stole a poor and innocent life, destroyed it, and made it bleed.
Speak up! Should you be allowed to continue to own this place and care for it?

Asking

As you stand facing one another, do you feel delight and
nurture pride?
As you stand facing one another, again and again, have you
lost self-control?
Do you insist on using that one precious thing you own for
that single purpose?

Do you plan and prepare for what will befall you in the
future?
Will you wait for the long darkness and the frightening
time ahead the way you've been doing?
When you see those who have been bounced about
tragically, what will you think?

If you do not want to revisit that time by turning back the
clock,
If you do not want to regret that time forevermore,
If you do not want to go down that path by turning back
the clock—

What should you do?
What must you do?
What?

Number

This is infinity.
This is not more than that.
This is a mask that
Tests,
Criticizes,
Suspects,
Opposes,
Confuses,
Calculates—
Greed and craving cannot be suppressed; they lead to
destruction.
Too much knowledge leads to pain and fear.
Follow no more, and be duped no more.
I hope that which even God fears will be used wisely.

A Thorn and a Rock

In the center of your heart are embedded a thorn and a rock.

If you are lazy, the thorn will grow. If you are born again, the rock will shine.

Raised by lies and injustice, a thorn is hidden amidst a thicket.

A rock, when vigorously polished with faith and diligence, can serve as a compass.

A thorn with deep roots cannot be removed. Hence, do not touch it or irritate it.

The rock that becomes a mirror to see yourself when you are born again.

It is your resting place and, when you lose your way and wander in darkness, a bright light.

It is a solid conscience. Through deep and vast thoughts, it makes your life abundant and gracious.

If you are not born again and do not polish the rock, it disappears and is overcome by thorns.

It turns into an impoverished and degraded shadow that trembles like a leaf.

If you fall from a cliff and struggle in a swamp, a thicket of thorns will blanket you.

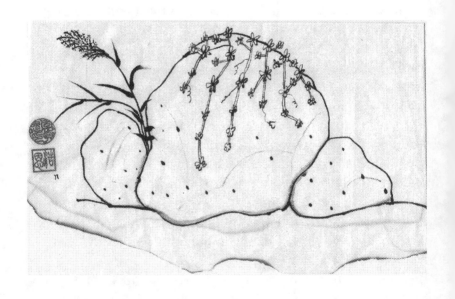

Center

New things
Good things
Beautiful things
Cool things
Excellent things
Expensive things
Unique things
Valuable things
Pretty things
Precious things
Special things
Old things
Coveted things
Convenient things
Necessary things
Useful things
Cherished things
Wanted things

Everything that is wanted is greed.
You call yourself wise, but you are not wise.
You have sold the self to greed and in return for a
scarecrow.
When greed grows unchecked and desire grows beyond
the threshold,
You become a scarecrow who has sold its self.
Protect and follow what is precious instead of needlessly
coveting other places.

Head

This is a complete tabloid edition.
I saw this and became very envious.
This blessing surpasses the imagination.
I saw this and understood your greed.
How those countless pieces
How those countless icons
How those countless signs
Came to be in your possession, I do not know.
But, I see you and think this is possible.
This is a beautiful, living, and moving amendment.
We must quietly lower our hands and become humble.
I cannot tolerate your arrogance any longer.

The Fourth Day

On the first day, the sun shone brightly, and the heads that
were lowered all about were raised up in radiance.
On the second day, the sun poured forth, and everything
became healthy.
On the third day, the sun continued to pour forth, and
everything burned.

On the first day, rain came, and the dried mouths all
around opened wide.
On the second day, rain came pouring down, and
everything squirmed with life.
On the third day, rain continued to pour down, and
everything crumbled.

On the first day, the wind blew, and everything around
began to dance in its coolness.
On the second day, the wind gushed forth, and everything
was blanketed by dust.
On the third day, the wind continued to gush forth, and
everything around was swept away.

On the fourth day ...

Degree

Laugh, and the whole world laughs with you.
Continue to laugh, and people laugh, rocking back and
forth.
Continue to continue to laugh, and they say you are crazy.
Continue to continue to continue to laugh, and they lock
you in a back room.

Cry, and the whole world cries with you.
Continue to cry, and people cry, rocking back and forth.
Continue to continue to cry, and they say you are bad luck.
Continue to continue to continue to cry, and they lock you
in a back room.

Greed

Wanting all things, I cast a net and got them.
The things that I had wanted so badly, I finally possessed.
Even those things that I did not want so badly also came
into my possession.
I now possess these things.
Things I wanted, I used well without longing.
Things I did not want are using me without longing.

To unlock all things, I used a master key.
Things I wanted to open so badly, I finally unlocked.
Even those things I did not want to open were finally all
unlocked.
I have unlocked these things.
Things I wanted unlocked, I unlocked without longing.
Things I did not want unlocked are unlocking me without
longing.

Rumor

There is too much talk.
That mouth ought to be kept shut.
Finally, with that mouth
Words that went in and out of a small door have now
opened all doors.
Finally, with that mouth
Words that went in and out of a small door have
brandished a knife and gone on a rampage.

Go Forth No Matter What

I explained it all already, but have reached this point
nevertheless.
It does no good to look back on the memories and glories
of days gone by.
We have no choice but to pass through this treacherous
place; we cannot pass over it.
Now is the time I hope you use the wisdom that you had so
very eagerly desired.
I hope you control your hearts and mollify your selfish ups
and downs.
I hope you face things with fiery courage, find victory
through perseverance, and go forth no matter what.

Words

It's so very difficult.

A wise person:
It was the first thing you uttered with your first cries after being born.
You had no choice but to expel it.
That which cannot be digested will be spat out and become thorns.
Therefore, that which is not swallowed but is spat out becomes a thicket of thorns that attacks the heart.
If we spit it out without swallowing it, this will lead to pain that cannot be stopped.

So why must we swallow it?

A wise person:
I spoke in a way that could be understood. Whether you digest it or spit it out is up to you.
It's difficult!

Experience

In the vast abyss of the sea, countless experiences live.
Some are big, fierce, and difficult to manage, but they give a
sense of being alive.
Some are small and beautiful, and through precious
sacrifice, make us love all things.
Some are still and slow, but provide sanctuary and
understanding of one another.
In that vast abyss, just when peace seems to last a while,
things suddenly become murky again.
Unable to resist any longer, greed lashes out and explosively
turns things upside down.
These things chase away idleness, which seeks entrance to
my vast abyss.
However, an abyss that lacks hardship and pain cannot be
pure, and hence, it grows toxic.
Oh, yeah!
Were it not for that salty experience, your vast abyss would
be but a rotting sea.

Your Coin

Your hand, which is said to be used wisely, goes
suspiciously in and out of the pocket.
You, who are said to be wise, take out all your coins.
It is curious why you take out the coins, which you had
hidden and cherished as if they were your very own life.
Have you, who are said to be wise, come to your senses and
decided to help someone?
Have you, who are said to be wise, repented and decided to
serve some cause?
Have you, who are said to be wise, regretted and decided to
provide some use?
Have you, who are said to be wise, realized and decided to
donate to someone?
At last, you, who are said to be wise, have started to melt
your coins.
At last, you, who are said to be wise, have started to put
your coins together.
You, who are said to be wise, have in the end, made that
absolutely pure coin.
Oh, headstone, come to your senses!
Oh, sleeping rock, awake from your slumber!
Your master is about to cross that line from which there is
no turning back.

Mother

The eyes of the two dark children are opaque.
I ask the children where their home is, and then take them there.
On the very top eave of a white, tiled pillar, there is a drawing of a mouse.
It is evidence that children once lived there.
There is no door.
One can see right in. Inside such a house, the children's father, who seems weak and crushed by fatigue, can be seen. From behind him, the children's mother, who seems embarrassed by the shabbiness of her surroundings and does not know what to do, gets up to greet me.
The children's mother hurries to build a fire and prepare some food.
With a tiny bit of almonds in a can, she cooks porridge, while the children scrounge up potatoes and cook them on skewers.
A smile appears on the faces of the dark children.
In a broken pot, the mother works hard to cook something.
I look closely and see an empty pot, in which black ash is boiling.
I see a pot that contains ash water.
The mother lowers her head as if she is sorry, even as the father turns his back to me, lying on the floor as if everything is cumbersome.
Mother, your shoulders must be heavy!

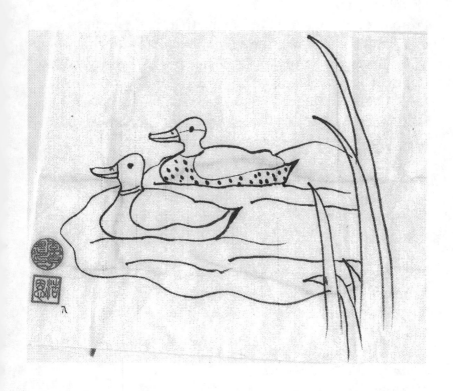

Fate

I am walking on an unknown road somewhere.
Walking on and on, my two legs are suddenly sapped of strength; the road turns into one of sand, into which my legs sink deep.
From the peak of a sand hill so tall that that it induces dizziness, I walk down alone, wrapped in my loneliness.
The hill is precipitous, but I struggle not to lose my balance.
But then, the sand knocks me over and sweeps me down.
The sand sweeps me along the sand road to this place, but there is no sand here. There are only rocks and pebbles in this landing at the base of a steep chasm.
A strange force surrounds me, and the water that springs forth all about is not common.
The chasm becomes increasingly narrower, and my footsteps and breathing grow more rapid from fear.
I have to get out.
I must get out.
A loud roar and the sound of a demon's footsteps chase me.
I run and run.
Ah! Fear and terror! Up ahead, I can see two underground tunnels.
Ah! I made it out alive.
I finally made it out alive.
I escaped from that place in one piece.
But then, isn't this place where I live?

Deceitful Mouth

Words never come out alone.
Words cannot travel about alone.
Words come out from two forks.
Words convey from the center of those two forks.
That which words cannot convey through curses is sent
again.
Curses, which were uttered lightly and in jest, now
transcend you and flow about on their own.
If it is too late and you cannot win over your words, then
bury them and let them rot.
If, even then, you still want to speak so much that you feel
you would lose your mind or life without doing so,
Then put a brick-sized hole on the lid of a large
1,000-degree pot.
When the first steam rises up through this opening, cover
it with your mouth, and vomit your words.
When your mouth becomes thus burned and melting, then
you will finally understand.

Warning

Because I loved you so, I had you, my most precious treasure, put in the most common place.
But, you were so careless that you have placed yourself in danger.
You, who continue to let things get like this with no idea about how to make things right, aggravate me so.

Because I loved you so, I had my most important rock put in the lowest place.
But, you thought so little of it that you kept burying it in the low place.
You, who keep belittling him with no idea about how to make things right, are in danger.

Pillar

Of five pillars, one arose and became known.
She who is said to be wise bartered with the demon.
Doing belated accounting, she wears dark clothes.
She who is said to be wise is attempting a transaction with the demon.
Another entity is bartering and, when done bartering, will also become known.
Because of those who are said to be wise, all will become known in the near future.
You are said to be wise!
But, because they are two, I do not worry.
These two absolutely cannot complete a transaction.
A transaction by two is something that even the demon fears.

Be Born Again

Bloom and wither.
Live and die.
Appear and disappear.
Fly and fall.
If you bloom, be born again.
If you live, be born again.
If you appear, be born again.
If you fly, be born again.
If you believe in yourself, be born again.
If you do not doubt, be born again.
Only when you are born again will you be recognized.

In All Things

Soil
Water
Air
Light
Love
Courage
Hope
Faith—
That which you truly need,
That which is truly important to you,
That which you cannot do without—
Speak of these things, and then speak more.
That which you seek exists in all things of this world.
But, in all things, there is a negative side effect.

Meaning

Build meaning,
But do not wave it around.

Build meaning,
But do not believe it.

Build meaning,
But do not be proud of it.

Build meaning,
But do not become familiar with it.

The meaning that you have built is your futile self.

An Opening

I try to enter through a small opening.
It is not something that was built after much effort.
It is merely a way to throw out the rubbish,
A mere conduit through which dirty forces travel.
You who have so much curiosity have found it again!
You want to enter it so badly that you cannot resist!
There is nothing I can do.
It seems you must always search for and know things to be
satisfied.
Go inside little things, big things, and gigantic things.
If all can fit inside, then hurry inside.
It is seductively smooth inside.
Fragrant oil flows so well inside the small hole.
It will be easy to go deep inside and fill it up.
But, should regret turn you around, the way out will be as
narrow as the throat of a flea.
Should resentment turn you around, your road out will be
filled with hardship and difficulty.
But, do not lose courage and do not ever give up.
Even though the opening is small, it is still a door and it will
become a road.

Dirt

Become friends with dirt.
Stones do just that.

Become friends with dirt.
Trees do just that.

Become friends with dirt.
Water does just that.

Become friends with dirt.
Flowers do just that.

Become friends with dirt.
Animals do just that.

Become friends with dirt.
Birds do just that.

Become friends with dirt.
Fish do just that.

Become friends with dirt.
All things do just that.

Filling in the earth, building fortresses, and constructing
towers …
You, who are doing things that do not suit you, please
return to your senses:
You are dirt!
Become friends with dirt.

The Best

What is the best?
What do you think the best is?
You say that what is called the best is the most good.
But, that which you call the best is not the most good.
The most good cannot become the best, and the best is not the most good.
No matter how much I think it over, I cannot accept your description of the best.
Think about it once more! What do you think the best is?

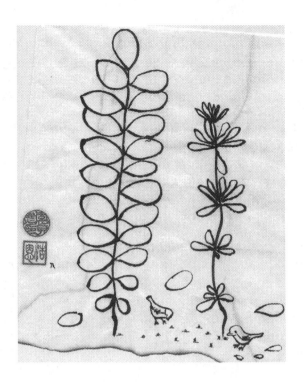

Dirty Things

Dust is going inside the flesh.
Grains of sand are going inside the flesh.
Wastewater is going inside the flesh.
Insects are going inside the flesh.
Dirty things are going inside the flesh.

To me
Various things came and entered the flesh, but they could
not pollute me.

Coarse things are coming out of the flesh.
Nauseating things are coming out of the flesh.

126

Bad things are coming out of the flesh.
Rotting things are coming out of the flesh.
Dirty things are coming out of the flesh.

Those things that truly pollute all come out from within me.

Nothingness

Do not cross the threshold.
That is the place where that fierce entity and the spinning sword of fire exist.
Do not cross the threshold.
Do you think that you are so wise that you can cross the threshold?
Do you think that you have conquered and have already crossed the threshold?
You have crossed something, but do not say that you have crossed the threshold.
When you realized that that place was not your territory,
You had already crossed over to a place from which you could not turn back.
Do you think there is nothing you could not carry out?
You may be capable of doing so, but do not say that you have done it.
Like a moth that jumps into a flame, it is not something that can be done without consequence.
Do not cross the threshold.
That is the place where that fierce entity and the spinning sword of fire exist.
Do not cross the threshold.

Mistaken Wisdom

Mistaken wisdom grows from dust, but, mistaken or not, it is packaged beautifully as wisdom.

It turns beauty into ugliness and precious things into garbage.

Like a drug, it blurs and creates addicts who waste strength on unnecessary things.

It controls my mind and fools my heart, pushing me to the edge of a high cliff.

This becomes that, and that becomes this. It sits as if it were the master of the room that holds my thoughts.

Carelessly opening thoughts has allowed this room to become the heart of the one who controls my mind.

Once mistaken wisdom is unleashed, it rushes directly into me.

Hence, open it not, but vanquish it.

Enlightenment

That thing called possession

Built fortresses
Constructed towers
Dug through mountains
Blocked rivers
Eclipsed sunlight
Removed moonlight

And became the master.

You, become enlightened. Stand up with wise thoughts and courage.
Let us topple and remove the towers and roads that you have built.
Now your thoughts and minds are flowing with purity.
Thought has become bright like the sun and heart has become warm.
It was also like this long ago. You have finally become enlightened.

A Thought That Is No More

In search of freedom and a dream, I climbed up the very high walls of a citadel.

Then I crawled through a narrow tunnel that connected to that place, and I fell out into a dark, humid little room.

Having pushed aside my hometown and risked death, I finally reached a heaven on earth.

As if I had been awaited all along, I was given clothes as soon as I was seen and told with silent eyes,

"From now on, you must live as I do. If you do not do so, you will be killed by those who hover about like air."

As soon as I received the clothes, my dream became an empty shell that faded away, despite my vain attempts to retrieve it.

Who are you and I?
Freedom disappeared.

What is this place?
Hope also disappeared.

What things happened?
Thought disappeared.

Beautiful Rock

The multicolored winds that have been scattered about the world are blowing, and unimaginable things are hurled about.
These things land wherever and confuse you.
They cleave, soar, and sink, and then squirm at sensitive and acute parts.
A dark force revolves around us; it is nauseating.
Wherever you eat, dress, and sleep, this thing lurks about and pains you.
Because this force swarms all about and grows full, there is no room for you to stand.
Sit on a low post, unlock the path of thought, and open wide the door to your heart.
The beautiful rock will thrash about in its will to live; it will cry out in pain and even seem crazy.
Your heart will feel as if it is about to burst and death is near, but it will calm down and grow peaceful again.
The long, long wait, which will seem as if time has stopped, will be difficult to endure, but you must endure it.
Endurance and waiting will be for the beautiful rock.
You a painful but beneficial antidote.
The beautiful rock will take care of you again, from inside the wound that does not heal.
It was injured and looked down upon countless times, but the beautiful rock will not forsake you.

The Difference of Thoughts

The fast thing is the slow thing.
The slow thing is the fast thing.

The fast thing is convenience.
The slow thing is inconvenience.

Convenience is harm.
Inconvenience is happiness.

Harm is a sweet thing.
Happiness is a difficult thing.

Have you ever tasted sweetness?
Have you ever tasted a fistful of honey or water cupped
inside two palms?
The sweetness of honey dries the saliva and parches the
throat.
Seeing water spill quickly through the gaps between the
fingers will surely drive a thirsty man to swallow foam and
roll about like mad.
That foam of thirst is a greed born of selfishness that will
suffocate and kill you.

Have you ever collapsed on the floor because things were
too difficult?
Did you collapse on water, which flows under the sun like a
jewel, or on the fine earth?

Do not remain unfulfilled, because things are as difficult and unbearable as death itself. Instead, shake yourself off and get up.

Everything exists around you—how joyous and wonderful! It is a difficult thing that requires strength. But, it will make you well.

Heart

That place, into which you rushed in a flurry, is a heart.
It is not another world.
Having settled there, will you now seek pleasure?
Having had even your spirit destroyed in a cruel fashion,
there will be no more hope.
You are residing in a place that ought not to have been
entered, so I hope you do not damage or dirty it.

If you accept without a word, lean your ears in and listen, and look to me, then you will be born again.
But, if like in the days past, you run amok in this place and ruin it through rash, thoughtless actions,
You will be cast into a swamp from which it is difficult to rescue even spirits.
You will be condemned to live on as a hideous monster.

Chapter 4: Meeting with Moo Ka Shi

The moment I feel an intense dizziness, I see that the place where I am seems to be my room. Father's face appears to me faintly. Soon Father's face becomes clear, and then I notice that another being seems also to be staring at me.

"Oh, Silly. Do you recognize me?"

Just as I am about to ask who the stranger is, Father's closed hand appears before me. Father's hand is always open. Now that Father's hand is closed into a fist, I find myself biting my lips.

"Silly, this is Elder Moo Ka Shi from the Won Ro Committee."

Father's soft voice comforts me.

Elder Moo Ka Shi speaks with a dull and grating voice.

"I hurried here because I heard from Master Moo that you were here. You're already all grown up now. You must be disappointed that it's taken me so long to come here like this, but please forgive me."

Father stares gravely at Elder Moo Ka Shi.

"Moo Ka Shi, Silly is still recovering and must be tired. So let us leave her in Jabez's care and go."

A very nervous Jabez is standing behind Elder Moo Ka Shi. He is trembling and staring at Father's back.

Elder Moo Ka Shi seems a bit disappointed by what Father has just said.

"Yes, let's do that, Master Moo!"

Then, his dull and grating voice turns into a sharp one.

"Ya Ru To Ka, give what we've brought as a present to Silly."

"Yes, Master Moo Ka Shi."

The one called Ya Ru To Ka, who answers in a thick, heavy voice, then reaches with long thin fingers to give me a dark red marble on which a blue cyclone has been drawn.

Jabez takes the crystal from Ya Ru To Ka and carefully places it on the table next to my bed.

Elder Moo Ka Shi, who with a cold smile on his face was on his way out, suddenly rushes back to me and grabs my hand. Then a strong force makes me tremble all over and I suddenly feel alarmed.

Elder Moo Ka Shi, who is trying hard to hide his surprise, says, "Silly, you have to pat yourself off and get up!"

Elder Moo Ka Shi turns and stares at Father.

"Master Moo, please allow Silly to attend the Won Ro Committee meetings from now on. Everyone wants to see her."

As if ignoring Elder Moo Ka Shi and what he has just said, Jabez hurriedly opens the door. Then Elder Moo Ka Shi quietly follows Father out of the room.

Jabez then speaks to Ya Ru To Ka, who remains sitting uneasily in my room.

"Master Silly must rest."

Urged on by Jabez, Ya Ru To Ka opens the door and leaves.

I am quite confused by the whole episode.

"Ah, this is ..."

"Hey, Jabez, what business brought Elder Moo Ka Shi here?"

Jabez opens the door a crack and then peers outside. Then, he slowly shuts the door with both hands.

"That brutal Moo Ka Shi must have come here to spy on Master Moo."

"Spy on Father! What for?"

"It's because of greed. I just don't understand why Master Moo leaves that wicked Moo Ka Shi to do as he pleases."

"Jabez, I don't know what you are talking about. Explain it so that I can understand."

The door slides open, and Father comes inside.

"Jabez, please go out."

Jabez winks at me and then leaves the room, closing the door behind him.

"Father, who is Elder Moo Ka Shi? And why did he come here?"

"You must be not be worried about Moo Ka Shi. There is no need for you to worry. Whatever the case, Silly, you must be not startled! From now on, there will be times when I call on you like this. So do not be startled."

Father is definitely worried about something. I want to say something to try to console Father, but in my confused state, I cannot form the words.

"I have startled you and made things complicated for you."

"Father, it is not like that at all."

"Whatever the case, we must hurry. Now go down and get busy on the itinerary set for you. Go and help them so that even one of them may be born again. Wake the rocks that are hidden and buried."

Father's two hands touch my feet.

"I will set out dark clouds so that you will not be seen and they will not know. You must go low under them like a small grain of sand or a small wind. No matter when and where, there will always be three eagles that will protect you."

Father touches my face with his two hands. Then, placing his two hands on my head, he speaks.

"Be born again."

Prior to the Itinerary

The only goal of the itinerary is to dream wherever I go.
If, by chance, you and I run into each other on the road, we
will not recognize each other.
I do not know how it will be, but we may inadvertently
even hurt each other.
Even so, I will go all around and then return to my original
place in peace.

If you continue your foolish actions, you shall go down a
road of thorns.
You shall spend unbearable days that appear to contain
only darkness.
How atrophied is all that you have done, and how precisely
precious you are.

When that which you launched grazed the curtain of the
hidden mirror,
That is your lot and you must each draw your own circle.
To do so, even now, you must be born again. You must be
truly born again.

Once born again, you will recognize yourself and will see
with faith.
You will see that which confirms love and peace for
yourself.
You will complete your itinerary and return to your original
place in peace.

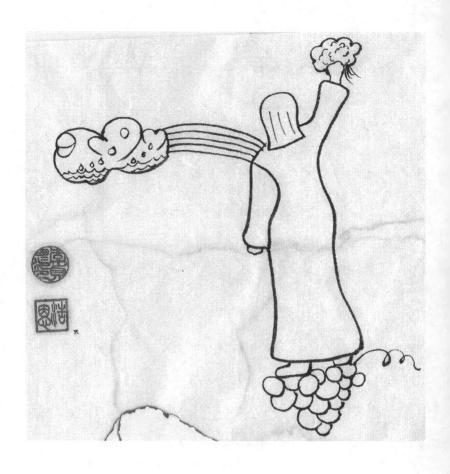